Cont

'Youth must go'

    – Anthony Burgess, 1962

Quotes

'The end of law is not to abolish or restrain, but to preserve and enlarge freedom. For in all the states of created beings capable of law, where there is no law, there is no freedom'

John Locke (1632–1704) was an English philosopher and physician, widely regarded as one of the most influential of Enlightenment thinkers and commonly known as the "Father of Liberalism".

Other quotes within the book are attributed at the end.

However, the original reference source is made to Wikipedia where necessary within the book.

Language

PIDPAT

The reader of *A Digital Tomato* should use the *PidPat* dictionary, which is included at the end, to read and understand the specifics about the speech in the book belonging to the local youths and gangs.

Language always continues to evolve. The Englishes spoken from Chaucer or Shakespeare's times to Dickens' London and then to the current day are very different from each other and very much of their own era.

Dedication

To all the youth of today and tomorrow.

May they find happiness and fulfilment in whatever they aspire to do or create.

Part I

'I shall colour my cheve red, today. Eh? Red nails too. Merky idea, ya get me?'

I bouche afo to myself in the mirror as I realise it had been so many days since I had gazzied or bouched to mouns. If I did not talk, mamot out fo nor sing from time to time, I thought to myself I might lose my larenks. The different new red colour allows me to alter my identity so easily. I feel so much better for the change.

I am the Respectful Raconteur of this dosye and I am not a writer really, but I will do my best to scribe as I panse, back and forth in time like it happens and happened, sisters. So firstly, I must tell you all about me. Then, I can tell you about my dilemmas. They are all extremely, deadly serious and so important to me.

My non is Henrietta, Henri, Enri, Rietta, Henry (which allows me gender gubble) Hen, Hal, Etta (my fave) or even Ta and sometimes simply H, but not often. The non which I choose depends on what I am doing, my mood and the image I wish to portray that very day. Most days I travat in my silo. I do not mix with gyaldem or mandem. The winternet allows this to trouve so easily. An email address and fone number for every non. Quite a chort. You will konprann in detail once I get on a bit further with the elaborate dosye and all the issues I face. They are fundamental to and make up my short lavi to date. I lack hope and aspiration as I sit here in my comfortable room. To be fair though, these four walls give me all the security I seek.

Today I am Henrietta. Naturally, before the colouring, I have black hair. I stand 5 feet 4 inches small. I am average build and with all my arms and legs attached. My zyes and zoreys work well, too.

There were other Respectful Raconteurs in my family, all trying to portray the same dosye. They were called lots of nons in their time, all pawol. Many of you may know them or even read their own labrish. My gran, Betty, a lovely and dear granfem, tells me I have many of their anreta traits. Gran Betty left home when she was young and was quite skrub in those ansyen days.

My fone pings just as I start telling my dosye. A wapp from Sally, my bestie, she is such a good blood.

'Chello, 8.00pm this night, at his yard. Says he is a fed. No need to check him out. I have his address, email and fone number and will send these to you, soon.' Her message says everything I need to know.

'Murder him boom,' I reply to this gal, urging her to have a good time and to seek a repeat performance, if she can. University is expensive these days and she needs to earn a living somehow. Better than nicking, I panse to myself. She needs me as her remote defans. I had done it many times. My reply was our code for receiving the message. I just wish her to have a chargin time and to keep safe. She deserves it.

You koumense to konprann me, my lavi, the dosye and all my hopes and aspirations. I had so many when I was younger. Let me first describe my room. My quas room is not in a tidy state. I do not like to keep it tidy. My lespri is tidy. I like things in their own compartments in my lespri. My kompyuter is on my desk, next to my bed. I always make my bed every single day. My parans are proud of me and particularly my degree at university. The only person in my family to get a grad and come back home sane. Cousin Billy frigged himself. Word in the family is he could not cope with the workload. He wanted to be a lawyer or some such silly travat. I never wanted to compete with Billy, plum, so I just got on with my kompyuter work and all that stuff. Taking the examinations with all that pressure was probably the first time I felt despair, real despair not as if I would snuff it but I could understand cousin Billy. Sally my blood helped me then, so it is my turn. All that stuff I learnt is such great fun now and put to such boom use.

I love my room. It is my haven. It is so secure. It is in my parans yard. There is a mirror where I admire myself and make sure I am not developing too many dark rings under my zyes. I need to take care in this department as I stay up late and keep very odd hours. I could develop a pot vant as I sit and sit and sit all day. I am gadeying at the kompyuter screen all the time, apart from when I answer my fone. I do have other bloods, mostly from university and we do keep in contact most days by the winternet.

My room is not full of ansyen patterned wallpaper, thank goodness. The walls are painted a pastel magnolia colour, so standard for the era. I have some Salvador Dali prints on the walls. They make me laugh and cry at the same time. The pictures create my own dystopian setting. They are mostly of the melting clocks he drew. He had a great lespri, quite fache. I enjoy all the surreal configurations which Dali drew and painted. Such wonderful pictures, if only I could match them. But I am much more mathematical and of course, musical. Gran Betty enjoyed classical music. I dig country and western music.

I told you earlier my room is untidy but I do know where everything is. I even have a real clock 'melting' in true Dali style to tell me the time. But that is not my pride and lajwa, believe me. I shall tell you what that is, next.

In between the items of fake Dali work I have the original prison number from one of my family. There it is in all its splendour, as I say, the original cloth. This is my real pride and lajwa. It is beautifully mounted in a silver-frame. I made sure it had the striped backdrop to reflect the garms he wore before his treatment. The dillbats. I am surprised he did not go fache, like Dali. Well, in fact I panse, he did. Gran says he was never the same and, of course, the family wanted nothing to do with him. He and his frers committed so many crimes, aggressive bodily harm crimes and some murders in those ansyen days. For what purpose? To clear and deal with their frustration, perhaps. The lack of any hope and aspiration for tinedjes must have existed in those days, too. My dilemmas are not original, then. This is not so new to me and my generation.

Reflecting on all of this and thinking about his own personal dosye has made me what I am, a true loner. But I have contact with so many with my kompyuter and the winternet, in all its world-wide glory. Also, I have my family living here which provides some comfort.

Pat and Mom always suggest bookcases to me to tidy my room. Since I recently got back from university with my grad they are on to me all the time. I agree it would make a difference as all my books, my personal bibliotek, are piled up in a corner. But the piles do not bother me. No one comes around to see me so what the hell? I operate alone. My soulyes and kreps are stacked neatly and I have a chest of drawers for my nezzies, garms and all sorts of things. Perhaps I am a lot tidier than I think.

Sometimes I open my bedroom window for fresh air when the stenks get too heavy. It looks out on to the garden at the back of the house and that is my real treat. The garden has trees, not a lot, but enough to give me some semblance of the season. The leaves provide cover and the green nature offers real comfort.

Gran Betty did pop her head in my room the other week. She says she appreciated the silver-framed montage to the family badman. This pleased me greatly. It was nice of her to say these mots. We have a fantastic relationship. I have nothing to prove there, with her.

I am 25. I was born in 2000. Gran was born in 1940 and Mom was born in 1970. You can understand, I am under pressure from Pat and Mom to donnen a baby or a bwoy. I am sure you can appreciate this specific dilemma, the pressure. It is to keep this donut dynasty going. I do not need that type of kaka, though, as a gal, it happens to be me they look to.

So, Pat and Mom and my brothers, oh my brothers, they ask me all the time why no boyfriends. My brothers ask, do I not want to be banged up? All of which I find very personal, indeed. Yes, I do. I have done it, but I found it messy. Most bwoys only want one thing - a bang. Then at first, they want to play with my tetes and get a tusky, after that I am supposed to make sure they get happy endings and it all basically distastes me. Such a messy business, as I say. I can understand it to procreate and further mankind but really, all that performance. Dye certainly filled stoodges up with too much testosterone. If that is all stoodges look forward towards, heaven help the future and all that stuff. Single minded kaka and they can okabine exactly where they want.

I will say again, stoodges tell me I am fit. This makes me feel good but it is always their opening line only to try and bang me. I would rather be ugly if that is the result of being so fit. I am a tomato. Chicks that sell their looks to the newspapers and mags really are cheap. Chungs is another word. Not using their brenns seems to me to be the way forward for women in the 21st century. The X Factor status allows them to be thrust into fame overnight for trying to sing. I do mean trying and bearing their moun, rass and tetes, always sells for good dosh. Sickening really, not for me. I have high standards, as you will see and evaluate for yourself.

My brothers are twins, born about five years after me. Left ekole now and are currently unemployed or rather unemployable. Taking their dosh off the state and recycling it back to the pubs and takeaways. One brenn between them but unfortunately neither is good at anything. Both have half of the one brenn which Mom put on offer when they were in her womb. I chort to myself.

I do have hopes and aspirations, but they get dashed at every turn. This government and every government, if you believe previous dosyes, all forget us jenn. It seems they never do anything to help us which can only mean they wish to forget us. Badmen in my book.

So, I stay in my room, very happy, very assured, but very alone, totally siloed. I do not need moun around me. With less and less exercise I am losing my shape, my outline is drooping and dropping. I really should care more. I need a plan for this. I really do.

Relationships bore me. So heavy, they are not my scene. If I want any pressing, I go out. Stoodges are simple folk. Some gal practice and they are all mine. Only failed once. Then I dump them straight after banging as they are recovering, still breathing heavy-like and telling me how good I was. I come home. I am Hen during those mess swas.

Today I am sitting in my red tracksuit. I feel so relaxed when in red. I have new brilliant white kreps, with a gold trim. They are just so cool.

I love some weed from time to time. I need it. It allows me to escape this mad world and all the depressive dilemmas I face. I make sure my window is open when I bun a brown, it is generally only once a day. The stenk of a bun makes the scent of my weeds disappear.

I also pass the time each day spending a few hours moni-
toring my jwet. I have devised A Digital Tomato. A computer
jwet which sits firmly in the all-time favourites for kompyuter
jwets. It is a simple chase. The players set out to find the pot
of Tomato gold at the end of the Tomato rainbow. Dystopian
because the players do not realise that every time a player gets
close, I extend the chase. Hilarious to con so many people especially when I increase the prize dosh, too. Social behaviour is
fun to watch. This could be the subject of my Masters degree,
perhaps. If I ever get the chance to study again. I have created
heatmaps, so I can gazzy so easily where everyone is playing. My
avatars are varied and many within each level of the game. They
allow me to interject the players' performance so easily. One
moment the avatar can be an ordinary citizen answering a question, perhaps someone in authority and on another occasion a
cute animal plucking at their heart strings, seeking consolation,
yet dangerously leading the player astray. My imagination runs
sovaj.

More explanation later about my study when I talk about my
grad, but it really is great fun devising my jwet. Keeps me interested all day long and I play from this seat, less than one meter
from my bed. I am creating such a simple life as all my dilemmas
concern me.

*The surest way to corrupt a youth is to instruct him or her to hold in higher
esteem those who think alike than those who think differently.*

I look up and the clock says 10.00pm. My bestie must have met
the fed, hopefully suitably remunerated, and I had forgotten to

24

check the stoodge out. I had better do that. I get on my kompyuter and look at the search engine for the non and match all blues in twos in the Midlands, which is where Sally studies. I need Sally to travat with me when she grads as she can develop and take my jwet into a chargin future direction, being the metaverse and Web 3.0. I cannot do this.

I type in the non and am quickly in shock. 'Kaka.' I must read this out afo. 'Inspector Bridgen suspended for misogynism.' I am showing sousi by now. I need to look it up in the dictionary.

Misogyny means '*a hatred, dislike, or mistrust of women, manifested in various forms such as physical intimidation and abuse, sexual harassment and rape, social shunning and ostracism.*'

'Kaka,' I say to myself again. 'I had not let Sally know.'

I read the article. 'Bridgen has been suspended from the West Midlands police force for a further allegation of serious misogyny to other colleagues. On this latest occasion he had actually tried to attack a fellow police officer while working late one evening in his office in the police station.' My word, these feds are a law unto themselves. I continue reading. 'Bridgen denies the assault saying he was encouraged by the female. The female police officer, who cannot be named, stated this was not the only time this had occurred. Bridgen had a track record and was suspended for a year. Bridgen had shown no remorse.'

On reading the report, I immediately panse of all the ways mankind has tried to and intended to change behaviour by various techniques. We have learned nothing in the intervening sixty years. The feds are to blame.

I think of my bestie. I have let down my frer so very badly. This new dilemma fachts me. I send Sally a wapp, telling her, but it was now 10.20pm. Is it too late? No answer.

I only have panses and dreams of her, there lying all tonni in front of this frig of a five-o.

Meanwhile, I sit safely in my room in my parans yard. Life candidly is not simple. It is all so unfair.

All she wanted was a pinky, perhaps even a bill. I start to cry.

2

'Anything to eat or drink, darling, it's late now?' Mom says. 'Left some salad in the fridge. I am about to go to bed.' I see it is now 10.30pm. She normally hits the sack earlier. It is late for her.

'Thank you, Mummy,' I say in a really endearing way between the tears, to let her know I still love her. She is after all, my Mom. I want to keep my relationship with her and Pat very solid and as it should be, in normal families. On reading other dosyes in detail, I feel it is where I could criticize moun and find fault. I need Pat and Mom, for the moment, until I decide what I want to do next and where I wish to live. This is one of my main dilemmas as I feel so crammed and unfulfilled staying here.

I see their door shut and creep downstairs to get the food from the fridge. Mom makes lovely salads. I could tell she cares about me. It is all laid out so neatly. The tomatoes, beetroot, patat mixed with salad cream, spring onions, a little ham and lettuce, so neat. Lettuce is so boring and bland, everyone puts too much on salads, in my view. I can't fault Pat and Mom's care and love. They just worry too much over me. I really do not know why.

Mom goes to travat in a factory. I am not quite sure what she does there, seems to spend her life packing goods, from what I can make out. I am not saying that is plum, someone needs to do it. It is just so boring boring boring. Goods 'ask to be packed' she tells me nearly once a week. Real donut sayings and answers to justify her simple life.

Pat travats at the bus depot. He drives buses and all that. Always pleased when they give him a new route. It makes his day or week. Also, boring boring boring once you have learned to drive and master one of those beasts. He had an accident about four years ago. He was beside himself. He kept saying his impeccable record was spoiled but it was not his fault. Or so he says. I do not reduce bus drivers to mindless morons, they do an important role in society, but Pat can do so much more. He does not stretch himself mentally. That must be where my brothers inherit their lazy genes.

I can zor them both asleep in their room. Pat is snoring heavily, poor Mom.

I get back into my room safe and sound, having finished the plate of salad. My brothers are not yet back from the pub. It is Tuesday swa so I suppose I should not judge nor give an eskiz for them on that one, they are actually adults now, believe it or not. They may go on somewhere and play cards at a frer's house. They will not be back until late, which means the house is very quiet. Total bliss. We live in Surbiton, South-West London. Our address is 25 Suburbia Road. It is a three-bedroom terrace in a reasonably nice road, a short walk to the shops and station. I am sure you can picture it.

I can now tell you about my grad. Also, my travat.

I am an A star student at mathematics at my ekole. Everyone looks up at me as if I am some genius dye. The mouns there, all the teachers and parans were convinced I would just go back into teaching. I wanted more.

So, I studied 'Legal Kompyuter Hacking' at my famous university in the Midlands. Coventry University, which no-one has ever zord about. What a great and tremendous subject to study. We all had such fun. Pyeing around with other moodies and their kompyuters. The professors were clever boffins. Mostly granmoun and a few granfem but in general very reasonable and nice mouns. I liked them all.

'Legal Kompyuter Hacking' is what it says on the tin. You learn the ethics surrounding the activity of making sure your system is impregnable. You also learn the good bits of how the badmen do it. You copy all of this and quickly become a hacker, yourself. I am. Serious, it has been amazing fun. Please do not think I am being frekan but I am probably the best in the whole wide world.

I am a kompyuter hacker.

If they discover what I am doing now they would shut the whole programme and the three-year course down. They, being the government, telling the university. Humbly, I scraped through and achieved first-class honours. Sally, my bestie, is in the year below, we met at a party and she came on to me, but I am not one of those progressive lesbies. She is clearly bi. I think uni and getting a grad drives you to that, mixed up lespris, full of worries, no dosh and too much work. Lecturers pumping you with leftie ideas and philosophies, draw available at every corner with social media coming out of every orifice and stresses galore. Poor kids, they need so much more cotton wool around them than they get.

My approach was simple, become a loner. Silo. Not involve myself on bewing to excess, all that drink and foolish behaviour. Have my escape trips with the weeds which were available and cheap. Nowadays, as I said earlier, I get mine easily, delivered at the local winternet drop-off centre at the petrol garage on the corner. Pat and Mom think it's medication. That is what I tell them. What a chort. I suppose it is a type of medication.

So, having achieved my grad, first class in that subject, what do I, this Respectful Raconteur, do now for travat, I zor you ask?

I continue to develop my jwet called A Digital Tomato. It is a simple chase through any terrain I consider worthy. I work on it all the time. The graphics are 3D, what else. Entry is £1. Millions have taken part because I hacked a few well-known celebs face-book and twitter accounts, so I advertised to their following. Such a simple calculation. I generally achieve about 1 in 5 new players for every follower of any celebrity under 30, 1 in 10 for those following under 40s and then it falls dramatically to be 1 in 20 for under 50s and I do not target the rest. It is not worth the hassle. Their followers are clearly not in to kompyuter jwets. So why bother. I target my hacking audience as I describe above and decide who to follow, it is a simple mathematical decision with algorithms. Created by me, of course.

All those komes trying to sing and become stars are worthy of my targeted approach. Models strutting around are great to follow. That is why I take the plum glossy mag each week following the stars. Do not want to miss anyone. Footballers and a few other sports stars are great meat for me. They do not have a clue what I am doing, they do not even know their list has ever been lifted. Others in the past would have had to lose a lot of time and dosh to get to this level of disruption in her world, in those days. It is just a few buttons pressed on my fave kompyuter and from my bedroom, secure and warm in my pyjams. What a blast. It really is.

The new words for this activity are 'key board warriors', 'shock jockeys' or even 'cyber raiders'. New nons are dreamt up all the time. Every month a new title and the non calling always depends on what and where you read or get your news. I am just a hacker, pure and simple.

My view is I am marketing and selling. Nothing illegal with this activity. My clients spend their £1, after all. I think about increasing the entry fee, but I hope you think I am clever. They have a prize if, and when, they achieve a new level, which is a bill. So quite a return which hooks them all in and they are generally young and a large number are students so this dosh is not so much valuable to them, but an achievement. Some want it, Sally wants it, I remind you. I wonder how she is doing.

The jewt is clever and while I have concentrated on rewarding my players with fungible tokens it is the new metaverse and the augmented reality where I want to take A Digital Tomato. Sally is an expert in this area. She wapps me with regular updates, bless her. The technology she is working on places data or inter-active digital objects within the physical real world as we know it. Then, with her help, we will be able to expand to non-fungible tokens as the prizes.

So, this next approach I am about to explain may be illegal. I have never asked a lawyer. When the innocent moun is one level away from the target prize at the highest Level being 10 (there are ten Levels in a section) and if they decline and want their pay out after a few attempts at seeking the prize and request their ini-tial investment of £1 to be returned, then they must return two Levels back. At that moment I am automatically notified. As it is effectively a refund and not an earn out, as it were. The jwet asks them to try again and make the rise to Level 9 so easy for them they obtain false encouragement and it automatically becomes impossible for them to rise to Level 10. I control the players. They are like mice turning on a never-ending wheel.

The chase goes into a loop so they cannot escape. They can return to a lower Level a few below, where they currently are, to try again. After a few attempts, generally about five, they give up. I have monitored this and the younger and higher social class they are the more chances they take, an interesting start to a social behaviour study, here. The posher the school the more they think they have a designed right to win. I take notes and monitor, all the time. I may start to preclude certain classes of youth, after all they have access to Daddy's dosh and therefore a good lawyer. This is one to monitor for the future with Sally.

Then if they take the chance to progress, they need to pay me another cockle and they can win a monkey or two. They forego the first prize. I am simply playing on their greed. A chello's greed never ceases to amaze me. As I write, I have only a handful of moun nearing the summit or highest level of this specific section of the chase, so I need to develop the next section. It is such fun. I have them currently looping at Level 7 of the ten in this Section and I need to release a few to 8 where they can make their decision. Such control. Like compliant little animals in a tunnel. The cheese at the end is the prize. I chort a lot when I analyse all of this kaka with my clever algorithms.

I let a few through to Section 2. At that moment I send a blanket message so all the players know it is possible. I give them £10. I want to restrict the pay aways and mint a new tomato crypto currency. If the players fail at this higher Section then they go into the same loop of kompyuter programming I devised for the first Section and they never go on to escape. They have just lost £1 to yours truly. No-one notices £1 but multiplied up to millions I do notice it piling up in my bank accounts.

The entry to the second Section pays me a cockle. What they win they repay for the pinky on offer at the end of Section 2. I chort to myself about the greed on display.

I am making lots of wedge. More later. One of my biggest dilemmas is I have paid no tax and I also receive government social benefits. Not yet repaid my eediat student debt. Working the system, like everyone else, give me £1 and I take £2, or even more.

The people playing are so different. Of course, I have a 'contact your Master page' and on occasions they do. The bare front of it. I am careful how I answer and again I give them a standard reply at first. If they are serious they ask again. Many do not.

'The Master has received your comment/question/query and due to the volumes of favourable comments we are experiencing we hope to get back to you within 10 working days.' Total lies, but how do they know.

Then if they chase me after another two weeks say, I send them an apology and a stupid nonsensical answer which they do not, nor will not, understand.

Giovanni from New York writes. 'I have been at Level 8 in Section 1 now for a month and see no way of getting out of it. Can you provide me with a clue – please?' A very reasonable and sensible question, obviously written in his nezzies and late at night, the nerd.

I reply. 'Giovanni, it is very nice indeed to hear from you. It is such a good question but please understand if the Master were to give you a tip or provide a clue then I am providing you with an advantage to all of those other players who are trying or have successfully achieved the Level to which you aspire. Please appreciate the principles and standards of high morals which A Digital Tomato applies with every player.' Quite brilliant, making them the fool, not me. Making them the sinner and not the sinned against. The Master's degree I yearn will be such a cinch.

I took the upper hand here and learnt it when I took a model on philosophy at Coventry. The university has an awful lot to answer for. I love my travat.

The entry to the jwet requires a form to be completed. This gives me the punter's non, address, email and fone number and then such details as age, qualification, experience, job and how they zord of A Digital Tomato. This goes into my programme and from there I can tell you so many details of the 1.5 million players I have already in play. In only six months, I have compiled that many. Genius. You can now do the maths and sums. I have quite a bank account with half of the players going to the second Level, over £8 million. What a chort. It really is.

I have broken the barrier to entry. I have devised the jwet. I am successful. But no-one knows. A serious dilemma. A Digital Tomato is nonned after me. A seriously attractive woman in this new digital age. It sounds good and proper, too.

With this dosh in the bank I could allow a few £1,000 winners or perhaps it may be worth my while devising a super bonus issue when they can multiply this up to £5,000 just by the player doing something special on Level 10 of Section 2. At that stage I can email all my players worldwide. Nothing quite like 'encouraging the others by shooting the admiral.' Who said that? Someone with a plum grill. I know. However, I really want Sally to come to help me as the future is the metaverse, augmented and virtual reality leading to this non-fungible token idea. I could create cryptomato.

The wedge which I have earned is a further real dilemma, I panse, and probably becoming a proper issue for me as I write this dosye.

Pat and Mom, I love them so much and they still travat like hell. They travatted extra hours to get me through university.

Perhaps I just owe them the university wedge they sent me. It was their decision to bang and have me. Not my issue, I was their dunfa until I was eighteen. I shall hold on giving anything to anyone, just now.

My brothers, as stupid as they are, do not work. Is it my moral duty to look after them? They are now adults. Do I share my success and give them lots of wedge? This would be wrong as it would make them even lazier. The only payback I can see from this course of action would be to allow Pat and Mom to be happy and thus to be able to ditch worrying about finances and, of course, fretting over my brothers. Another dilemma for this Respectful of all Raconteurs.

I like being on my sel. As I have said before, in my silo.

Then there are my frers and a few besties. Such as Sally, oh Sally.

I turn away from my beloved kompyuter, where my world begins. It starts there and never stops. My lespri is already starting to wander on my choice of activity and hence my new non for tomorrow. Such a choice.

This was my main dilemma. I had all the dosh in the world that I required and was hiding it from everyone, family, bloods and frers.

Suddenly, I realise, I have not yet received any reply from Sally. She normally earned her wedge only once a day. She is not a chung. I should expect a wapp tomorrow, I thought. Perhaps, I should give her some wedge so she would then not have to meet those nasty stoodges particularly feds like Inspector Bridgen. If he is a real five-o, that is?

36

I wonder.

Bed, dodo and dreams now. A welcome rest to such a busy day. So much more fun to have tomorrow. Dilemmas do not occur in sonjes. Nor do they get resolved, unfortunately.

Sally working with me, chargin.

3

I wake up thinking about Sally, the eediat chick. She had not sent me a second wapp with the old Inspector's details. Never mind.

Today I am going to be Etta. It is jwet development day.

I get out of bed and take a shower. I was not too fo and my brothers did not wake up. Luckily in this quas yard we all keep different hours. Pat and Mom at travat. My brothers asleep. I can raid the kitchen and find some healthy munch. It works well and as we do not gazzy each other too much, then there is no bataying. Only when we make something and another moun eats it. Such as my zes which seem to disappear on a very regular basis.

Back to my room and some thought for the next Section. I need to keep these punters, sorry clients guessing and your Respectful Raconteur earning good dosh.

I shall set out the jwet in detail today for you. You will see it is such great amusement and something players do on their way in to, or out of ekole, university or even travat. They can pick it up or put it down and freeze their Level. This is so they rejoin where they left off and do not fall back. Subtle mental coercion in force, here.

It is a simple chase and the players once they have paid their £1 get a lot of fun from playing it. Effectively therefore, I earn my £1. The whole jwet to date took hours in development and as you have zord already, I stay one or two Levels above my players. I track and trace how they are doing, what mistakes they make and alternatively how they get from Level to Level. This enables me to think through the creation of all the further Levels in each Section and enhance all the previous ones to make it harder and harder. Sally even mentioned wearables to me. Such as an attachable digital tatt. Technology is moving ahead so fast.

For example, lavi is all about algorithms, now. We are all just a number in this great wide world. How often does the teribla mainstream media quote loads of numbers back to us on the news when they try to convince and talk to us. These statistics, numbers and percentages are all over the journals. The numbers all mean nothing and the media read so much into them. The media make up any dosye they want to. All the wrong ting, all the time.

The feedback I receive from players is they enjoy my jwet. I am so pleased. I still call it a jwet, however, it is my travat, really. About 15% currently playing have been recommended by their friends, who play. The first Level is gentle. It takes them through familiar ground, like a home setting. We all like this. It comforts all the players and as the first Level is easy, as well, it provides them all with a sense and feeling of achievement. Simple manipulation on the players' mental approach and playing with their aspiration, again. How clever am I? They escape via the chimney as the fire takes hold. If they save any members of their family the players score heavily and can accumulate those points to accomplish arriving at the next Level. Babies saved from their burning cots are treble bonus points. I am building in realistic social awareness in this particular play, you can evaluate and judge for yourself.

After their home, or a stereotype of a western home, I lead them into the garden and have created all sorts of animal dens, play areas and a little 3D imaginary sport to play. Creating some nature and all such things provides consolation and mental reassurance. I have received rave reports for this Level and again the achievement to the next Level is relatively easy, in my opinion.

After the garden we go to more rugged terrain, taking the players away from their comfort zones. No eskiz there. I need to stretch them and allow them the panse of achievement. In the deepest valley with searing temperatures, I question how they are to survive, then in an ocean and finally they go to the highest mountains, from there they embark into space and are asked to live on make believe planets. My imagination runs away with itself and quite honestly, I would prefer Sally to work on this as I have said before now to you. She is so much better at creative arts. Now, we are at Level 10 and the serious questions get raised; do they want to go on to the next chase? Bribed with the thought of winning more dosh? This is when I do not allow them freedom of thought, they are under my total control.

Old Giovanni from New York was not the only one to ask, but my answer seems to have shut him up, at least. Terrific. I was vit there, also very compelling. His sousi was well answered. Wait a minute, a wapp from him.

'I understand your concern but if I pay my entry to the next level surely that means I can escape. What if I commit to this new level now? Giovanni, NY.'

A prompt answer is required now. 'Giovanni, lovely to hear from you once more and thank you for taking the trouble to contact the Master again.' A quas bit of stroking his soul and a sob story to follow. Goes a long way with these malen nerds who somehow mache their way around this world. 'If you pay the entry fee to the next Level then you have not earned it and could be cheating yourself. This is not the way A Digital Tomato wishes to encourage their patrons, their clients and or customers. Ethical participation is essential to our core beliefs.' Clever, eh? Should keep him quiet with such a vit and complete retort. I play the moral high ground, once again.

Suck on that Gio. I got you by the bubbles, I panse to myself. Satisfied. Exactly what A Digital Tomato is not, but who cares or even knows outside of this silo.

My real dilemma is how to handle the dosh I earn, not the pesky players.

The dosh keeps coming in. I have opened so many bank accounts, it is unreal. I do not want any accounts earning interest. I know the nasty taxman gets reports of the accounts earning interest from the slimy banks. They have systems that match the account and the taxpayer, to gazzy if the chello have reported the very same. These days, this needs a lot of careful administration by yours candidly.

The law abiding and merky mouns of you out there, will think I am wrong. But let me tell you more about my thinking.

The government do not put their resources in the right areas. Currently, in my view all or any state intervention encourages poor behaviour. It is all down to behaviour. Look at me. I am earning secretly in my quas room in my dormy. I bother no one. I take my benefits because they are available to me. What poor behaviour is that? I could pay off my student loan, but why should I? I seek help from the health service when I get my period pains, which are heavy each month, I can easily seek good protection and assured advice before I have a bang at the week-end. It is all on a plate for me. So easy. The wonderful national health service has made us unhealthier.

I repeat poor social behaviour is encouraged.

I do all this stuff, which is questionably wrong, because it is there and available to me. Everyone does it to some extent. The government, in my respectful view, have taken the thinking and responsibility away from each individual chello.

Plum in my view and the leftie do-gooders are asking for more. This is not sensational stuff. It is my thinking and a few of you out there will think I am so right wing, I am a nazi. I am not a nazi, I do not go around killing innocents, willy nilly. I am not punk either. I ignore chatrooms, where I can. I have no cultural powers of persuasion over my neighbours nor print journals saying the same. It is just I believe in the rights of the individual and most importantly to give hope and aspiration to the jenn. Oh, my sisters, my sisters, my poor eediat twin brothers. If you look at them as fine examples of the production of 21st century Britain, then we are losing it, big time.

They are gubbled. They have no ideas what they can do for travat. The state gives them some wedge each week. They have no ambition and least of all any plans to seek for what to do next.

Will they get a job? Probably not. Will they marry? Probably not. Will they have a family? Probably no. What does this lead towards? Frustration and badmen, in the making. Chellos just like those before them repeating again and again, and all over again.

Giovanni wapps me to say thank you. Good he has gone away and continues to loop in Level 8 of Section 1. He deserves it. I shall put an alert on his jwet. If he looks even close to escaping and elevating himself to Level 9, I shall loop him again. He can be the perennial hamster in the wheel, such control. Such lajwa in my travatting day.

This rant of mine leads me on to the political classes. They do not have a clue. I read it once some politicians do not know the price of a pint of good old lait. A famous quote. History is littered with many quotes because when Gran Betty was jenn the old man said, 'You have never had it so good.' What BS is that? Back to the cost of a pint of lait, it is probably because their team, staff, researchers, secretaries, little helpers get the lait for them. Eediat politicians, have no clue.

Not spending my tax wedge appropriately really fachts me. I earned the wedge and it is mine to splash it about, as I see appropriate.

The welfare budget they keep talking about confuses me.

Dosh for being homeless, dosh for being unemployed, dosh for the sick and the pregnant. You get dosh for anything. You need very little pride to claim. Just fill in a form present yourself to the office and wedge is sent to you. I do it. It is easy and painless. They hand the dosh out. The action by so many cannot be considered fraudulent. I do not have a job, but lots and lots of bank accounts. All digital and all passworded. I have an algorithm to donnen the passwords. I am just the Respectful Raconteur of this dosye. I really hope you are learning from me all the time.

I do not want to be a dunfa and will make sure it is all disclosed when I meet a partner and donnen a chick or bwoy. Then and only then, shall I straighten up and smarten my act. It will be then at that specific moment in time, which I choose, when I shall join all the other mouns in this messed up society.

It will be then I shall buy a property, a yard. It will be a boom yard and well deserved. Then and only then I shall sit Pat and Mom down and tell them about my travat. Their reaction will be interesting, to say the least. They may be facht or they may be pleased. It will be what it is. I shall become a right real capitalist, such an upstanding member of society, too. I have never been punk and will not start then, either.

By killing off any hope for the jenn and giving them no travat means the government can control all the young. That is my take on it. Create poverty and then the military will take control and take power in every country.

Time moves on and no wapp from Sally. Might have been a longer session and more wedge than she expected. Perhaps a monkey, even. That is good news for once, I am happy for her.

45

From time to time, I do feel trapped, perhaps depressed, whatever that means. I consider it means I have no hope nor aspiration nor for everyone else. I confuse myself on this one. Depression means contrasts. My life consists of these four walls, safe, secure and a comfort zone. I am making dosh as I have explained and I have put myself in the very good position but I cannot declare this to anyone, nor spend it. Hence, I feel depressed.

I need to be more fulfilled, the real power I have over my clients is not enough.

Pat and Mom may be right, meet a bwoy, donnen a family. Continue the same old cycle. I need a real cultural interest. Where do I find that? When all I do is exist and live on my own?

Some lesser than me have jumped on occasions after treatments. I am not high enough here in my bedroom. I need to find a higher ledge. Bad thoughts do pass across my lespri.

Firstly, I shall send a wapp to Sally. 'Hope you left him finished. Wapp me when you can. Do not forget the sharp screwdriver.'

Secondly, I do not need to find a higher ledge and jump, just yet. I have the next section to work on, after all, A Digital Tomato fulfils me so much. It really does today. I am OK.

Thirdly, I need to create a better relationship with everyone.

I think of all my sisters. Oh, my sisters. Especially Sally and all the future possibilities we could have with Web 3.0.

<table>
<tr><td>

4

</td><td>

I sit here contemplating so many more thoughts about today's society and in particular how I, your Respectful Raconteur fit in. Your very Respectful Raconteur.

</td></tr>
</table>

I am a chick. A merky chick. I like to think I am a dam. I aspire to be a dam. However, the more I read in the mainstream media about dams in the big wide world the more I despair.

They let themselves down. Chicks and dams are not good. Believe me, I am one of them, too. They abuse their sexuality, like Sally, my bestie, and then cry wolf whenever they can. The donut tomatoes.

Look at recent crimes committed by famous women. The world is fascinated by women who kill and those who appear outwardly normal before striking. Nurses, such as Beverley Allitt, Jane Toppen or carers such as Rose West, who act from a position of advantage.

The female form and prettiness beguile the press, media and of course the suspects. It is candidly ugly. Gender simply viewed like this is a virus in itself.

Then they use their sexuality to become predators. Women have the advantage and can turn their cold activity on or off. No flowers in the morning and it is perceived a crime. Of course, from time to time it goes wrong. I am Sally's defans and it makes me feel good and important. There are particular movements to protect women, but they should help themselves first. Not use banging as a weapon. I wonder if I can introduce this into my jwet, for men and women and then work out attitude from an algorithm. Something to really think about when I get some spare time. That will be the day. My own crusade. What a chort.

Then there are all sorts of other issues and problems in the world. I skirt around them and can ignore them from my room, comfortable warm and no stresses. But lots of personal dilemmas exist, for sure. I have told you about them.

The political classes, the wrong Leaders, Heads, Presidents and Prime Ministers. Completely unqualified for the roles they play. Democracies which fail. Racial inequality, I cannot be bothered to be so politically correct in my own dosye. There, I have said it. Previous writers have not been correct on many fronts and not suffered. Immigration is good, very good when controlled. But no UK Government understands that. It is a free for all out there. I like my four walls.

Cancelling people is the new war waged by the rebellious classes. They take on anything their protest group wishes. In the end their targets do not exist, but they do have to go through a few months of humiliating or celebrated disentangling of their persona and CV. Quite disgusting in my view. The cancel culture must be stopped. I know I cannot do this alone. I can start and Sally can help. I need to seriously think how this can be engineered into my jwet. Perhaps Section 4, by then I can incentivize people to do the right thing and motivate them to think for themselves with a stunning prize. Etta will not change the world on her own, but she can damn well try. And I know I will try.

If I put my head above the parapet, I know I would say the wrong thing and be cancelled but the one weapon I have, not buff nor banging like the others, not brute strength either is that I can probably out hack them. After all, I received a first-class degree in hacking, legal or illegal, no matter what.

A wapp from Gio. 'Struggling to move to Section 2. Help please?' I choose to ignore this.

I turn to my music. Such a comfort to me, it is unbelievable. I mentioned before my taste is country and western. I like the big nons, of course, I do. The big 'O', Roy Orbison. His voice such a remarkable sound, like an angel falling backwards through a window. All the greats look up at him, Elvis, Springsteen and Dylan amongst many. 'You Got It', 'Only The Lonely' and 'Pretty Woman' amongst so many hits. Perhaps my favourite is 'I Drove All Night' such an experiment with escapism and trying to find a piece of heaven. I love it. I play it over and over and over again and I know all the lyrics. I wonder if Gran Betty likes him, too. I expect so. Same era.

Then I turn to the man in black. Johnny Cash, so troubled and yet so masterful. The others Willie Nelson, Merle Haggard and Charlie Rich. There are places for some of the chicks, too, like Tammy Wynnette and Dolly Parton. A medley of all their songs is something to behold. The best of country and western can engage me so beautifully as I sit here and devise my programmes, all the Levels and the devious chases. I escape. Inspiration is not the word to describe my feelings, there has to be another such as exciting or motivational but the music in the background certainly enables the creative juices to run and to flow so extremely fluently.

Then there is a knock on the door. 'Come in,' I say without thinking.

The door opens and my fraggle brother, Cyril is standing there sheepishly all efreye. If I had to choose between the two brothers, it would be Cyril I would favour. He has a modicum of more sense than his brother, Albie. Cyril is tall and thin. He always smells of booze because he spends most of his hours drinking. I had not yet approached in my own lespri the panses and fact he may be starting to border on being an alcoholic, but I was certain he was going that way. Could I or should I do anything to help? I am not so sure. He was an adult and always liked to tell me this when I spoke with him. He has long straggly brown hair. Unkempt and very unattractive. His face is pock-marked and I must admit I had not been out with him in public for some years. His clothes are a T-shirt and jeans. He possesses old brown kreps, too. He often wears no socks around the house and luckily, he did today. Otherwise, that sight of his long feet and toes would have turned my stomach. Cyril is not a smart nor even an attractive specimen of the human race. He also seems to boss his twin brother around. Both decidedly unpleasant characters, but they are my family.

'Hello. Just one of you?'

'Albie is still in bed. I am going back there soon. I went to get some lait. This letter was downstairs for you.'

Why my parents had nonned them Cyril and Albert is way beyond me. Perhaps they knew they would be dumb losers and the nons suited them, even at birth. Cyril hands me a brown envelope. It is addressed to me. It looks important.

'Is it important?' My brother always manages to state the obvious.

'How do I know until I open it.' I give a truly obvious answer... back to him. Not a brenn between them. I say to you my sisters, oh my sisters, they are plums.

Cyril turned and goes away leaving the door open. I get up quickly and shut it behind him.

I slit the envelope open. The letter is addressed to me. It is from the nasty, avaricious and greedy taxman. OMG.

I shudder and shiver at the same time. Quite scazzy. The brown envelope made me like that. All official. On Her Majesty's Service. I shrug my zepols and open the folded paper, here we go. I read it to myself.

'Dear Sir/Madam. We are writing to you as we believe you may be working and we require details of this income to update our records. The details should show, your employer, their reference number, the rate of pay and, of course, any tax paid to date.' The cheek of it, I panse to myself. How intrusive. All I am doing is minding my own business and playing jwets. I need to consider how to answer this letter. A quick and immediate reply will put them off the scent.

Etta, nothing to hide. Just reply.

I decide to go downstairs and see Pat and Mom. They are having their meal in the kitchen. It is a Wednesday early evening and they had both been at work. Pat worked shifts and Mom decided to get some overtime pay while it was on offer leading up to a busy summer season. She must pack goods for customers in need of summer ranges. I should find out what by asking one day.

They look up and smile and as I had not seen them for a week, I smile back such that my grizzle hurt.

Pat says. 'All OK with you, Henrietta?'

'Yes, fine.' Answered in a slightly sarka way.

'Good.' Came the reply. My Pat did not use many words.

Mom can't help herself. 'Isn't it about time you moved out, dear?' I panse the 'dear' was an afterthought to finish her sentence.

Why?' I am razwa sharp with my retort.

She looks shocked. 'Well, Henrietta, you are getting older and surely need your own place and life and things. It is only natural.' She tries to justify her words to me and to herself. I wonder if she is concerned there are no bwoys around me. I panse to myself what the hell she meant. Then, 'It is in your own interest, get away from us, your brothers and start to make your way in the world, dear. Dad and I really do love you.' The last sentence seems so unreal. It definitely feels false and to me lacks any genuine feeling whatsoever.

I am embarrassed. This was the first time she has shown any emotion to me for years. Perhaps since the pesky brothers were born. Why should I listen to this frig ting now? I had too much on my plate just now. Developing the next part of the jwet, above anything else.

She adds, before I can reply as she was not quite finished just yet, 'we both want the very best for you.' Sure, they do I panse.

This is emotional blackmail and just what I do not want right now. My own parans turning against me. Chucking me out of their comfortable yard. Just as I am settled after university. To me they had me as a baby, proud of my grad and they should not shirk their responsibility to me. Me, their only daughter and eldest child, at that. This will add to my depression. It is right now with everything else going on when I should be on the lookout not to add problems in my lavi.

'How long have I got before you want me to move? Weeks or months?'

'Take your time, dear.' Pat adds all sarka back to me and so condescending. 'The boys can wait.'

A little bit of attitude clearly derived from Gran Betty, probably, comes over me then. I want to aggie the stoodge. I refrain and give him a gade he will remember for a long time. I am not up for bataying in the kitchen of my own yard.

'Thank you.' I turn and go back to my room. There is no need for any further conversation.

Another serious and most immediate dilemma. The eediat brothers who are no good to anyone, neither man nor beast, are being given housing priority by Pat and Mom over your hard working, loyal, affectionate, street legal, honest, delightful, sweet, caring and kind Respectful Raconteur.

Fairness does not exist as a word, through any thought nor action in this whole wide world of ours. That is so very clear to me now.

Nothing yet from Sally.

<table>
<tr><td>

5

</td><td>

I retire upstairs to my room without displaying any emotion, whatsoever. As soon as I shut my door, I burst into tears. Again. The emotion of rejection has been with me since my brothers were born, when I was

</td></tr>
</table>

about five or six.

This clear manifestation of their demonstrable care for me, or lack of, hits me hard. Very hard. Pat all smug sitting there relaxing with his pantoufs on. Mom looking at me with love, so hollow. I could see they had planned this attack and were leaving me with no option but to fly the nest. I was giving them what little wedge I could from my benefit dosh to make it seem realistic. I admit I had not delved into my earnings from A Digital Tomato, yet. Perhaps now was the time. If I do, I shall need to write a reply to the nasty taxman, first. I should possibly give Pat and Mom an insight to my winnings and earnings. So many dilemmas, turning into bigger issues and possibly problems, for yours candidly. Choices, dilemmas, issues and now very real-life problems.

I come up with an idea. I will search for rented accommodation in this street. The very street I have lived all my life. I know all the local shops and have everything organized for my online delivery, especially all my weed and spliffs. It would mean I can still cadge some meals from the notoriously happy couple downstairs. Still see my brothers. I am fast becoming very delusional with my need to stay in Surbiton. Albeit such an advance from my Gran Betty's modest abode somewhere in North London. The alternative and it may be best for me, is to go far away. Become aloof and elusive. This is another dilemma. Is it an issue or perhaps a problem now? I need to think it all through.

I open my window, lean out and have a brown. Next door's chat is playing in our garden. I shoo it away and it runs under the fence. I enjoy the stenk from the brown, it is so very soothing when taken at the right time.

Once I have stubbed out the brown, I go online and see some properties. They are decent enough. One such opportunity is a room to let and only three doors down the road. Very good value and even affordable off my weekly unemployed benefits and wedge which the measly government give me. I apply.

Seeing this vision and potential outcome, I am able to pull myself together. I zor a bri. There could be some movement from my brother's room. I pop my head outside my room, they are both going downstairs to the kitchen. Cyril leading, as ever.

I follow them into the lounge. Cyril enters. He holds a large cup of tea. It being early evening and all that, it is wonderful they have decided to surface from their pits.

'Hi, sis.'

'Hi Cyril.' I was ripping at first. Then I try to engage with him. 'Why don't you call me by my real non?'

'Well, to be honest I don't know it.' Comes the eediat reply.

I never give him the credit for being quite such an embesil. Nineteen years old and still not understanding all the family dynamics, such as our nons.

'Henrietta, if it's helpful to you.'

'Yes, I know that bit. But lots of other people call you other nons, all different, like.'

'True.' I confess. He seems to be latching on to and understanding my identity crisis. Has he been listening into calls I had made recently? Has he hacked my kompyuter? Or is he watching out for letters addressed to me, like the recent one? Perhaps none of these but just a confused jenn stoodge.

'So, I call you sis. Easier. I discuss it regularly with Albie. He agrees with calling you sis.'

I am now of the opinion they are inseparable. They have had too much time in the past growing up in their tinedje years living, breathing and sleeping together. I remember the teachers telling Pat and Mom this was going to be a serious social problem for the future. Pat and Mom just blamed circumstances, the small yard and the lack of opportunity for the boys to express themselves as individuals. I recall, Pat and Mom referring to the teachers of the issue their older sister was a dominant and overbearing force. The hate and personal cancel culture started then. The fact the twins had to be taken to class and all their other activities together, as it was too much hard work to separate them, all the excuses roll out, including blaming your Respectful Raconteur.

'Sis, we understand you are moving out.' I question to myself, is this a done deal then?

How did he know this? I wonder to myself? I have just been told and they have only been in the kitchen for a fleeting second to make the hot cup he is holding with his thin fingers and with his fragility, it looks as if he will drop it any moment. Clearly these plans have been set for some time, I conject. Not my sousi, any more. I am moving onwards and upwards and, of course, out of here. My lespri is made up now, if it hadn't been before.

'What makes you think this?'

'We asked Pat and Mom if we could have your room. This being a three bedroomed house and all that.' The twins speak tinedje but Cyril seems to have drifted into adult English and even between the two of them, for the while anyway. Perhaps to make his point and sound more important, influential, manly and the like.

'Cyril, you asked Pat and Mom?'

'We both did. It was not just me.' Cyril tries to correct and backtrack. 'For some months since you came back from university we have felt, well, cramped for want of a better word. Our style stalled. I know you konprann.'

'I didn't know you knew such big words.' I am all sarka with him.

Cyril lets out a broad chort. He drinks his cha.

'When do you want me to go, then?'

'No rush, sis.'

'Thanks very much. I shall need to look on the winternet at potential properties. Do you think I should stay local or go a long way away?'

'Up to you, depends how you see your future.'

I look at Cyril. What a chort. The grisly, thin and ugly bedren lecturing me on the future. If I were to ask him the same question, I am sure he could not even make any comment about his activity tomorrow, let alone any time in the future.

'In all honesty, what do you see your future to be, then, now you mention mine,' I retort.

'Sis, Albie and I have no jobs. All the jobs are now digital. The manual labour stuff is there but so hard to get. Only a few available these days. We do not want to train and learn something new. Finished that at ekole. We want no responsibility, we just want to turn up, do what we are told, earn some dosh and come home. Much like Pat and Mom. Their jobs for example, Dad's driving and Mum's packing are few and far between, you know that much, surely? As important as they are.' Cyril is politically correct and respectful to his parans. An admirable trait, indeed. His only one.

'I do. You are saying there is no hope, then. No aspiration for you two and therefore no hope.'

At that moment Albie enters the room. I have not seen him for a few weeks. He looks even thinner than I recall. Albie is as thin as Cyril but not as ugly. A paler complexion makes his brown hair look darker than Cyril's. They are both the same height and often mistaken as each other. I could tell them apart as Albie's face is not as pockmarked and his nose fits his face better.

Cyril was just simply plain ugly. Albie would pull chicks for sure, despite being dimmer and having less conversation than Cyril. Cyril, because of his looks, will be a loner all his life, I am so very sure of this fact.

'What's up, sis?'

'Her non is Henrietta, Albie?'

'I knew I opened a few items of post by mistake, didn't I?'

'It was you,' I say accusingly. 'I thought it was Pat or Mom.'

'It was me, I am the badman. Don't knew where you got that £20,000 from? In that foreign Spanish bank.'

The little dillbat had opened and read my post. Perhaps I should leave this house before they find out too much more about me. Sisters, my brothers have always been a pain in the rass to me.

'Prudent behaviour, over a number of years. They call it saving.'

'Cyril and I cannot save at all. Especially on the small amount the government give us. It all goes down the pub and if we have any over, we seem to lose it on the jwet of cards we mess after hours.'

'Very progressive, you two. No hope nor any aspiration.' My sarka tone hits home.

'What chance do we have, we don't understand the need for qualifications. We left school, we can read and write.'

'Just that. Read and write. High bar.' My sarka tone hit a stronger note. As a firm retort comes from Albie.

'Look I am fed up with this conversation. Just let us know when you are going. We can hold a party. Have a few mates around. You do not have any friends. You may fancy one of ours, after all. Young stoodges, you know the score, sis or don't you like bwoys?'

I leave the room. No answer was given as it was not deserved. It is then I make my final decision. I need to move a long way away from this set of losers. All of them. I am strong enough to do it.

Pat and Mom were lovely, hardworking in their own right, but clearly they feel an obligation to this set of moronic twins they had donnend after me. The obligation was such I am completely shunned. Again. Cancelled in my own yard.

Everything I think about my generation and those younger than me was true. No hopers, the lot of them.

I had better start to look for a flat. Big decisions ahead. Do I buy a flat, do I incur the wrath of the nasty taxman and become a proper person? Enter the capitalist regime, now or later. A big call.

I return to my secure haven. I look out of the window as the night draws in. My lespri was made up and I now needed to write my reply to the taxman. I know I cannot ignore this any longer as it was eating away at me. I know the alternative will be they will start to write to me again and again, chase me and make my life hell.

A quick review of A Digital Tomato. Only a few players at a Level they may need to go to another Level. At Level 8, about four, including the infamous Gio from the even more infamous New York. Such a nerd. Still beavering away. He had not given up. The eediat. Is a £1 entry fee so important to him, or is it pride? Something Cyril and Albie do not have. About six at

Level 8 of Section 2, still looping. No questions for the Master. I have time to search the winternet for a property.

Firstly, I need to choose where I am going. Secondly buy or rent, and thirdly what do I really want.

This jolt and rejection from my family can turn to my advantage. An opportunity for me. Get away from the drudge and dull life this last six months have given me since university finished.

Tomorrow I am Henry. This life must be made to be fun, as hard as it is. Well done, Hen, practice what you preach.

Bed, some dodo and a few sweet dreams. Still nothing from Sally. How strange. I expect she has a terrific and fun dosye to tell me when she emerges from this somewhat unnerving, quite unusual and eerie silence.

<table>
<tr><td>

6

</td><td>

I wake up to the bri of the front door shut-
ting, in fact, slamming. It must have caught
on the wind. It is Thursday, so who has gone
out, I ask myself. It must have been one of
the teribla twins. Cyril always seems to have

</td></tr>
</table>

more character about him than Albie. He is the leader of the
two. If I were to force myself to make a choice and seek a favourite between them, it would be Cyril. I am always wary about
Albie, a little deceitful from time to time, opening my post.
How dumb. As if I do not see through it. If it is Cyril, who has
left the yard, he may have gone out for some of his choice munch.
Fast food and chips.

Clearly, I am getting extremely bitter after yesterday's con-
versations with my brothers.

I am Henry today. An influencer and Emarq magnet. Master
of the winternet bidding wars. Cyber warrior of great repute.

Today is the occasion I turn my attention to answering the
taxman and finding a flat or yard. Somewhere to park your
Respectful Raconteur's rass and her wonderful kompyuter
gysmos. De gran events in my lavi to date.

Albie knew and of course, he would tell Cyril I had some wedge. It surprises me they had not asked for any. Perhaps they will do so just as I am leaving the yard for the last time. Then they can avoid me on a daily basis, possibly shirking responsibility of any repayment. Sisters, I am getting so much more mistrusting, of my own brothers, sad. Look after number one, Henry, I say to myself. I do not like the non Henry, but it is OK for Emarq trading. Makes me sound like a stoodge if I wish it to. A good cover. Some realignment.

The taxman, first. This nasty, avaricious and selfish group of people. A total drain on society.

I read the letter again. Why do we always think them as stoodges, nasty stoodges. Wanting every moso of you.

Big dilemma; do I buy a flat or a yard? My first purchase must be seen to be reasonable and based on any earnings I may have made in the last six months. I think to myself by holding £8 million in various accounts fully declared would lead to a batay with the fraggle taxman. The cost would be too much and too high and the overriding issue to the wrong mouns and for the wrong purposes.

Yours candidly seems to be kenbe in a circle, closing in on me. All coming at me at once. I need to think. I look up at the wonderfully silver-framed picture. I look at Salvador Dali's melting clocks. I look out of the window to the trees blowing in the wind. They all give me inspiration. I listen to the big O and the man in black. I have enough in me to fight all of this, break through and win.

I can tackle this and be victorious. I have an idea. I can beat all this kaka.

'Dear Sir or Madam,' answer them with the donut address they gave me. It was signed off by Mrs Dharsanny but I choose sir or madam. Nice and impersonal, shows they do not bully me. I do not crack at this, their first letter.

'I recognize your request for my recent details and earnings.' Get to the nub quickly. I must make it seem there is no flannel. 'Therefore, I thought I would advise you about my one-off winnings from gambling and betting. I have been following the horses for some months now and about a month ago I put £100 on an accumulator and won £250,000.'

Yours candidly has worked it out. The bet would pay this amount at Newbury for the Saturday's winnings. A bill placed correctly would net about £252,461. Enough for the public uncovering of the cold habit. 'I would like to take this opportunity to claim travel and expenses against this amount, but it would possibly make it a trade or profession, so I decline this opportunity.' Humility, they will surely fall over themselves with this approach. I read about it on the winternet. Who needs a pesky accountant or tax advisor?

'Also, I feel I should mention this is not a habit. I have not gambled since, so I am not only not hooked but also not addicted. Accordingly, this is not a trade nor a profession as a regular means of earning. Therefore, it remains untaxable. Thank you. Yours faithfully, Henrietta.'

Let me read that back. Reads well. I would believe it, so they should, as well. Must mention my degree and mathematical prowess. Those facts will add to my ripping, fair, impartial and neutral approach. Highly credible. Your Respectful Raconteur, yours candidly has pulled off a masterstroke here.

'I need to advise you that I was a first-class mathematical student at school, with A star grades and a first-class honours degree in computer work at university.' I shall leave out the hacking bits. Too much information. I chort to myself.

OK. Type it up properly, make it look professional and proper like. Put my address at the top and sign it. I have not written a letter, or snail mail, they call it, for so many years. Probably not since I applied to university. I need a first-class stamp and can pop this in the post later when I go for a walk. I need some bits from the corner shop myself. I shall not ask one of the twins to post it. They will not know what I mean. God help them.

I will never zor from the taxman again. You cannot pay tax on a one-off win, as I mention. Great day at Newbury. I do not need any travel tickets nor proof I was there. I am not claiming these. Perhaps some photos would have added to the case but these days this should be enough. I really should not overplay it. I can show I made my wagers online with a simple backdated hack. This wonderful new digital world, all at my finger-tips, right here in my bedroom.

I see Mrs Dharsanny has an email address. I expect she does not use it. The nasty chellos in their tax offices are years behind the jwet. I expect I shall need to explain horse racing to them and what an accumulator bet is all about. They should get out more. I am not being frekan, again, merely factual.

Henry the product influencer and Emarq magnet is insurmountable while in this mood.

Ping. 'Still looping and not progressing. I have tried everything. Just putting you on notice this jwet is a fraud. Gio.' Strong words, my stoodge. How has he worked that out? He is a real nerd. What cheek what a front, he has?

No need to answer this, let him stew in his own juices. See what he says next.

Then an immediate ping. 'Will be taking you to court. Giovanni, New York.'

All for £1, I pause to myself. The stoodge is an embesil. Take me to court. The whole point about the wonders of A Digital Tomato is they are all individual players. One of my first history books at school mentioned the words, 'divide and conquer'. Exactly how any government deals with the population in any country. The governments play them as individuals and as loners who cannot fight back nor argue. Brilliant stuff and poor little Gio wants to take me to court for a £1 entry fee. No other losses are evident. This is hilarious. No mention of the fun he has had playing, nor thanks for the work I put in to make it all happen. I am tempted to goad him on the poor little eediat. But they are everywhere, embesils in every walk of life.

Like Mrs Dharsanny will be one, too, when I have finished with her. That is, when I have finished with her good and proper. Gran Betty's friends would have given her a beating. Looking forward to the future dialogue, I will post the letter shortly, Mrs Dharsanny. You just wait Mrs D.

'Gio, it is such a shame the entertainment you have had from playing A Digital Tomato is not considered worth £1 but you see it as just a money-making device to win your £10. I have explained why I cannot provide you with a digital lift into the next Section. That solution creates an unfair advantage. However contrary to the game's rules, I can return your £1 as a one-off goodwill gesture. The Master.'

I must try and get him by the bubbles, hurt him in some way. The non-fungible tokens Sally can devise will be attractive to nerds like Gio. Worthless really but so different and unique then the players will want them, especially if I can authenticate them as proper cryptomatoes.

'Gio, with respect we must draw your attention to the rules written by our eminent UK lawyers.' You guessed correctly, yours candidly nicked these from another digital jwet. 'Each player plays at their own risk and are prepared to lose their bets, as if it is an entry fee to the deep, fun and enthralling digital scenes within the game as well as all the mental challenges. The Master.'

I wait before I go into Emarq. No reply. Hopefully, Gio the giant New Yorker has ducked himself from my world. Cheeky dillbat. He needs to stoke a few other arguments to have a go at me and my rules. I wonder who did draw up those regulations.

Emarq is an interesting digital programme and easily hacked. I did not dream up the concept nor write the programme. It was such a good idea, and another death knell to the high street retail shopping experience. However, the programme was so susceptible to people like me. I wangled the bidding each time so that I stopped all other bids being received by the recipient and then my bid, however low or unrealistic wins the goods. I act as an early adopter as I monitor the type of item I wish to trade in the marketplace. I block other bidders. I create a scarcity in the bidding war by redirecting the bids to other goods, they do not want. I see the complaints. What a chort.

Then I sell the items on, after an appropriate time, to the bidder who wanted them anyway ahead of me with their higher bid. Hilarious digital manipulation. What a great hacker grad, I am.

There were clearly some facht buyers and sellers out there. If only the taxman could see the inner workings. So many trading here on this platform and all of them not paying tax. For that, I am sure.

It is really an unlevel playing field in respect of tax and government spending. That should be my next piece of research. On a mundane layer I must concentrate on this Emarq business.

It is a fun day while my own digital jwet builds up. Quick look another 200,000 players this last week. Over 82% have been recommended by their peers. That is £200,000 to me. Pat and Mom, Cyril and Albie have no idea of the success of their donnen and sibling, the mighty Henry, Henrietta, Etta or whatever I am.

Do not care much for Henry. But as Henry I can troll Emarq and buy a few goods to resell at double the price, she is quite a girl. My golden rule is no more than double otherwise someone, somewhere may pick me up. I also wait a few days or even weeks for everyone to forget my purchase price. Just in case. There are so many eediat stoodges out there across the winternet.

Too many hackers in my simple opinion.

Then there is the darknet, and I do not want anything to do with that world. Draws, chungs and total corruption. Why go there and advertise your crime? All the nasty badmen hang out there asking to be caught. Everything I do with A Digital Tomato is on the winternet.

This badman does her business with such subtlety, no-one can catch this hacker. Gio, the taxman or any trader on Emarq.

Your Respectful Raconteur forges onwards and upwards with great triumphs all the time.

My degree was fun to do and gives me a chargin career.

| 7 |

It is Friday morning and I wake up and decide my non today is Etta. This is because I am going to develop more Levels for my jwet, A Digital Tomato. Also, I wish to establish and evaluate the numbers of players in the various loops. I must work on these algorithms and provide a few with easier paths to enter Section 2 and Section 3 once Sally works with me. Only fair, after all, and the algorithms will show me the more people who are encouraged and how they are encouraged the more they could urge their peers to join. I love it. I love the control this gives me.

Later today I shall work on some of the concepts in Section 3. The Level above the one I devised a month or so ago. It must be futuristic as Section 2 was primarily war jwets and similar such situations. So, a little intergalactic warfare and animation would create a very plausible diversion from the softer start in Section 1. Yes, I like this. It shows progression. A little bit of bataying and some nicking to get on to higher Levels. This outline took a few hours and enabled yours candidly to escape my current woes of gading for a place to live. I can even introduce a pandemic into Section 3. My bestie will love this space to create.

How do you as a person or government deal with a pandemic? The worse kind of pandemic needs to kill children. This will make people think hard about the coronaviruses we have suffered recently just accelerating granmouns and granfems deaths by a few years. The tinedjes were unaffected. Yet the economy got screwed, big time. This perspective really will make people think.

I gazzy the pictures on my wall. The melting clocks from Mr Salvador Dali give me true and deep inspiration. My panses wander. It is pure escapism and such fun programming. An outline is enough for one session, some further programming later in the week.

Then suddenly I panse about Gio. Where is he? From my quick review of Section 1 Level 9 there are now 162,318 people playing or in my view, struggling and only 5,308 have said they will go to Section 2. Gio is somewhere in there. I find him, there he is, no activity for twelve hours, he is one of the 157,010. Poor, little Gio. Too difficult for you, I question. No emails to the Master in twelve hours. I have won. The 157,010 can continue to struggle, for the time, anyway. I will not help them, yet.

As soon as I am satisfied about Gio, my thoughts turn to Sally. No word or wapp from her. Enjoying herself too much. Perhaps Mr Bridgen, the disreputable fed, was still paying. Monkey after monkey after monkey. Good gal, my bestie.

I should give Sally some proper dosh. Get her out of this demeaning downward spiral. It can only end in tears and my donation will allow her to concentrate on her degree. She will make a great business partner. She possesses some brilliant strengths and chargin attributes. Mainly being the ones which I do not have. Ideas on the metaverse, Web 3.0, the play-to-earn games market, virtual reality, crypto currency, blockchains and the like. She has a great imagination and can build more sections and chases, while I concentrate on the business side of things. Handling the dosh. Particularly the future earnings.

Next time we are in contact I can let her know my thoughts and see her reaction. Decision made, she is a good girl and needs help. I would rather help her than the de teribla embesils known otherwise as Cyril and Albie, my brothers. Oh, my sisters, how I wish I could talk to you all for guidance.

I go out for a walk and post my letter to the taxman. I take the opportunity to look at a few of the properties around here. It confirms my decision to move away. Move away from dear old Pat and Mom. As good as they are, we all need a change. It will give Cyril and Albie a change too. Allow them some space. Then, I can ask the question why are they not working and trying to get on in life? Set them some targets and talk through their progress, but so much easier from afar. There, another decision made. What a memorable day so far.

So what area, a little further out from where we are? Currently located in South-West London, means going towards Guildford. Sounds great. I can buy a flat. Sally and I can work from there. Three bedrooms, one for us each and one as the office. Chargin. I am on a roll. It is all fitting into place and working out.

I do not want any embesil stoodges around me. No babies, yet. Might get a transfusion of sperm later in life. I have years yet. Let me have some fun with Sally and see where my hacking gets me. Soorted.

I might get pregnant with a little Henrietta, by mistake. I would not want to live with any stoodge, though. The dirty bwoy dillbats are always in the way. The ones I met at university put me off them for life. Drinking beer, being sick, farting unnecessarily and watching football. Not my 'cup of cha' as they say in my parans' kitchen.

I arrive home from the short walk, let myself in and go straight to my room. I have a takeaway coffee with me and could enjoy that for the rest of the day.

Looking for a flat in the Guildford area on the winternet was my priority, but I could not help but look at the mainstream media news.

'Body found in Coventry area.'

My stomach turns over. Sally. Surely not. My beloved new partner, my bestie. A body found in Coventry area. I can barely make myself look and read on. I have a very deep and extremely uneasy feeling in my lespri. I have not zord from her for a few days, now. Most unlike her.

'A body has been found in the Coventry area and police are offering no further details about the case. They need to not only advise the family but also follow up on the first leads on the case. Accordingly, a news conference will be held tomorrow morning at 10.00am.'

I need to read on. I have to see the further detailed reporting.

'The Chief Inspector said to our reporter. "While the public may need more *information for their own and continuing safety, we must treat this with utmost care, as a killer is potentially out there. While we believe this case is not linked to other cases, we recommend no one goes out after dark alone in the Coventry city centre and wider area tonight and for the next few evenings." We shall update you on this news stream with any further information, just as soon as we can.'*

This is so candidly efreyeing. Awful. My bestie Sally. Is it Sally, it must be?

Sally was playing it to the edge, earning her dosh from testosterone filled stoodges by satisfying them. The result for her was always the end jwet. With pride she could get by and fund herself at university.

I feel so terribly guilty now. I am useless as a defans for her as she plied her trade. I am nowhere near good enough. Really sisters, I have let her down.

I burst into tears and cry and cry. Again. I am totally unaware how long I am in this state. Why was life so hard to just live? Perhaps Cyril and Albie have it right. Pat and Mom just go to work, come home, eat and go to work, a never-ending boring circle of life. A life which Sally has no more.

My zyes are now red. I wipe them. I look in the mirror. I look shocking. They match my hair. This fachts me more.

The front door closes hard, I could zor the bri. It must be Mom back from work. Time have passed me by.

It would be difficult to start to tell Mom about this, I must keep it to myself. I am not sure if I mentioned Sally's non to them anyway. If I did, it would have been just as a good blood I had made at uni. When I first arrived home they often and ritually grilled me about my experiences and the people I had met.

Probably checking I had not met anyone bad, who I might bring to their yard.

I certainly did not tell them about the bwoys so perhaps Sally was only referred to as a decent chum and blood. There was no need to bouche about her after I left uni. My grad was the whole matter of my concentration while I was there in Coventry and I had lost touch with so many of my local frers. That is the line I need to take. Of course, they may not have picked up the news, just yet. No need to worry.

Then there is a knock at the door. I look at the Dali clock. It is 6.00pm, late for guests. Who was this knocking on our door? Why am I so nervous and edgy? The news had completely thrown me. For once, I could not think nor amazingly work on A Digital Tomato. I am not in a good place.

Faintly, I can zor words and my Mom bouching with someone.

'Henrietta, dear.' She shouts upstairs.

Who wants me? Perhaps they have left and gone away leaving this lovely, yet dysfunctional family of mine, all alone.

'Yes, Mum.'

'Someone here to see you.' This is an invitation to go downstairs and meet this someone.

Is this a trap? Who the hell wants little old me, yours candidly? Gio the plum, the nasty taxman, my bestie Sally, but she's dead, Sally's family, my teribla brothers, any other sisters, someone who has discovered my dosh, dear Pat or anyone else I may have recently facht. A long list. The local shopkeeper could be in this group for all I know for I nicked some of his stuff. Perhaps even the local delivery man for finding my weed in his van.

I look at the wonderful silver-frame, then to the Dali prints. I think of him and all the anguish he suffered at the hands of the authorities just because he was mad. History cannot repeat itself, surely.

Just, before I go downstairs, as I gather myself and I make sure my mug looks presentable, I think of poor Sally. Her body found in a ditch or something equally as disrespectful for the end of someone's life. A life so short, so unfulfilled and yet with all her future hopes and aspirations taken from her.

I think of every other young person so let down by the system and the authorities.

I open my door and trip quietly downstairs into the kitchen.

I could not believe my zyes. In the kitchen there in front of my very own zyes are two boys in blue. Two boys in blue in all their glory, next to Mom. Their glarbies, sparkling, pressed and looking so formal. Holding their hard hats in their hands. The very dillbats. One a chick and the other a bwoy. I presume the chick was present because of me being a gal and all that. Then no hanky panky can be carried out and no accusations made on account of incorrect or poor sexual behaviour. The chick is there to ensure fair play on this and every occasion. Fully understood by me and nothing left uncovered by the boys in blue. Dillbats, the lot of them.

'Henrietta, these nice police officers want to speak with you.' Her mug was full of anguish. She has offered them cha and I zord her say sik, but neither fed takes her up on that.

'Thanks, Mum,' I turn to the boys in blue. One so fig his vant stretched the buttons on his glarbie. He then accepts Mom's offer of sik. Understandably to get his vant even fatter. What a wasteman.

'How can I help you?' I ask, so politely and with such measurement for one so young and innocent, I panse.

The chick fed speaks, supping her cha. 'We wish to ask you some questions and want to take you down to the police station to do so.'

'What is this about, officer?' I continue to speak in a calm and collected manner. Sisters, you would be proud of me. It could have been considered almost disrespectful but said in such a way with a lovely smile to offer true decency and politeness to these dillbat jakes.

'An incident in the Midlands with which we feel you may be connected, madam.' The fed adds.

'Well, it's a bit inconvenient tonight. Can I come down in the morning? And as I have done nothing wrong, I have been here all the time, haven't I mother?' Mom nods. 'Then, surely you can afford me that arrangement.' Yours candidly adds with assurance.

I really did not want to start to identify Sally's body tonight. It is only a few minutes since I read the news, after all. I was not ready for all this, I was scazzy, actually. I am inwardly so sad. I don't know how I hide my shaking. Really very scazzy.

'That is a matter of conjecture.' The fed chick is quick to point out with equal assurance to me and with some frekan, which I do not like. An accusation in my view. I let it pass. I do not react.

I smile. 'Look, I know my rights.' BS generally baffles brenn. 'I shall come down in the morning, it is late now. I have work to do.' I gadie at Mom who is looking very surprised at my forth-rightness, if not extremely proud. I could tell so from her mug.

'OK, we shall place a guard on your house. We do need to interview you tomorrow.' The bwoy fed compromises with me while the fed chick who had an annoying gade on her mug just listen and agrees, I could see with difficulty. I could knoprann why there would be a guard. The feds did not want me to run away just in case. It is not a cuss.

A defans on my own front door. Only Prime Ministers, Presidents and Royalty have that respect and kindness afforded to them. I felt so extremely special.

At that second, l reflect about Sally and her tragic demise. Inwardly, I am in turmoil. I want none of this. I feel totoy.

We agree and they leave. I have a lot not to look forward to. Overnight house arrest was going to be the least of my concerns. I go to my room and do not speak with Mom. Pat would know soon, too. My brothers were out but would know as soon as they arrived home from the pub. They would have to pass the officer while blotto. I just hope they do not have any weed on them, but that would be their problem. I send them a message to tell them to be careful tonight. Typically, no reply from them.

A win for Etta against the feds. A night at home. I go to kab-icha but I am very very very sad about Sally. I am.

I am not looking forward to what tomorrow brings. Not at all.

Poor Sally, who was my bestie and was to be my future business partner.

Part 2

I

'I shall colour my cheve yellow, today. Eh?
Yellow nails and beautiful matching toe-
nails. Merky idea, ya get me?'

I wake up earlier than normal. I have a
difficult day ahead. Identifying Sally's moun
will be such an unpleasant business. It is then I realise all my
ideas to develop A Digital Tomato into the metaverse will have to
be put on hold.

I need to take some time out to do my hair and present myself
well, it will certainly take my lespri off all these matters. I know
for sure the feds will be here to collect me at 9.00am. They will
be prompt with no badmen to catch at this time of day. Taking me
into custody is such a simple task for them.

Early morning hunger takes over. I pop downstairs and grab
a sandwich. I can zor no-one else is up, awake and about in the
house. I do not want to gazzy anyone anyway. So the emptiness
in the house is good news. I just hope the day continues like this.
My lespri is clear with what I have to do. Simply identify Sally,
tell the jakes what I know about her, her family and what she did
at university and return home. They must know my number

from her own fyon and the wapps we exchanged. The whole episode will surely take an hour at the most. I will be back in my room out of harm's way, in no time at all. There must be others to interview and meet. Her regular list of clients, perhaps? Some of them may be there being interviewed as well. I certainly do not want to meet them. The dirty dillbats. I really hope the feds know I am this innocent little bystander, helping a friend out. On reflection, therefore they must respect and treat me accordingly. I am not so sure the five-o understand this sort of language and they treat everyone the same as a violent badman. I do know the feds train in violent conduct. Perhaps previous tinedjes laid the ground for this approach. My lespri is awash with all sorts of panses. Keep it simple and straightforward I zor myself saying.

Back in my room, I collect a few things and put them in my handbag. My credit cards and fones, all of them. The fones go into a secret compartment underneath the main bag. This allows me to only show the boys in blue the one they know about. I am certain they will not search me. You can never be too sure, though. They do like that sort of thing. I think it makes them feel entitled.

However, I have no lock on my bedroom door and I do not trust my brothers. I am sure they will enter my bedroom and snoop around, while I am out of the house. They will not be able to keep their grizzles out of it. This is the main reason I work such long hours. I am of the opinion a lock would make them think and then grasp the fact there is something important or valuable to discover. I asked Pat and Mom some months ago and never had a reply. This means to me they were not keen. I have not bothered to chase this up because I am always here, but I am going out now for an hour, my brothers know I am out and detained, and I really hope it is not a moment longer.

'Right, I am ready.' I zore myself say. The time by my Salvador Dali melting clock says 8.55am. One last look and touch of my silver-framed picture in all its pride and glory. I love you everyone and Gran Betty, here we go, downstairs to hell.

No-one up still, not even Pat and Mom to say good luck, not least goodbye. Charming, perhaps they really do want me to leave this fowzy yard. If this is the subliminal message to me, I receive it fo and clear. Do not worry. I look around at the bare hall, it only had one table with a few eediat bits of china which I thought looks like rubbish adorning it. Pat tells me Mom thinks they are valuable. Mom has no taste. Pat never cared about those pieces. He always uses the excuse 'we can't afford it', if ever an upgrade around the house is mentioned. So negative. I open the front door.

The designated fed, both mindless and useless is outside and standing to attention, just as I expected. For what, I do not know. Perhaps just to look good to her associates and bloods in the car on the road. A chat runs down the path ahead of us. Next door's, it jumps on to the wall and runs away. We open the front gate together, yours candidly and this chick. Her mug is all formal, no smile and nothing said. We both know what is required.

The police car is white and shiny with a few stripes and one jake in the driving seat. One of the rear doors is opened by the fed chick and I sit in the back. The fed chick gets in the passenger seat and off we go. A nice comfortable ride. I feel like a dunfa.

85

If we stopped at lights, trapped, I could not get out. The doors are locked and controlled by the dillbats in the front.

I look at their glarbies, no hard hats worn in the car, not even the flat ones. They would not fit in with their big tets. I read the numbers on their zepols. A letter and three numbers for identification. They had obviously been programmed. It is a journey in complete silence. I remember their numbers, I panse to myself it may be important for me in the future, but probably not. Not sure why I thought this. Perhaps an element of self-defense, kicking in. I must admit this silent fifteen minutes in the back of the shiny five-o wagon taking me on the way to the station is a very unnerving experience. I cannot nor will not recommend it to anyone. Yet, I have done nothing wrong, how weird is this? It makes you feel guilty just sitting there.

We arrive at the police station. It is greyer and less commanding than I recall. I had only walked past it on occasions going to Gran Betty's new house, the other side of town, since she moved from North London. The officers alight the vehicle, they politely help me out and show me through reception with a nod and a wink 'here she is guv' and then I am being shown into an interview room. It is warm but empty. Two chairs either side of one bare small desk. One internal window from which you could only see in. In contrast this room made Pat and Mom's hallway look superbly and tastefully furnished. I have not said anything to anyone yet, during the journey or while here. Everything has been put into effect by hand signals and motions, all very strange. The feds seem to have lost their larenks.

86

I sit down and put my bag on the floor next to my feet. It is heavy with all the devices inside it.

They make me wait a few minutes. What is this all about? If this is how they treat the innocent then how the hell do they treat the dunfas, those who have done wrong? Badly I can only presume. I am never surprised with anything I zor about the five-o. Because of things I have read, all very well documented in various narratives, I am very doubtful indeed. But I must hold an open lespri. What travat is this mindless stuff? Perhaps Cyril and Albie would fit in here well. What a chort. They have no brenns at all and it seems everyone here just follows the rules. I suppose the more senior the five-o rise in this odd hierarchy the more they can operate as individuals, but even then, there will be rules and regulations.

I start to think who else is here. I realise Sally's clients were almost certainly all in the Coventry area not South London. Well, I presume this to be true. Surely, they will not be here, in fact it is quite a trek to bring Sally's body here so perhaps I shall not need to identify her limp dead carcass, anyway. Good news. It may be just a photo, but if this is the case, why not at home. I must just be here for a simple interview and to tell all on how well I knew her. Where is everyone? I look at my fone. I have been here thirty minutes already. Is this their way of showing their importance and to show a superiority over the blameless? Keep everyone waiting. How boring and what a waste of time. I could be devising Section 3 by now. I could be usefully programming. More importantly, I could be counting out my dosh.

Then the door opens.

In walks an important looking bwoy. He looks serious. He does not have glarbies on like the other feds I have met. He is dressed in a smart, grey suit, a white shirt and blue tie. His hair is cut short, I think it goes with the travat. His aftershave is very heavy and quite sickening. It wafts in ahead of him. Very distasteful. I hope Sally did not find Inspector Bridgen with the same awful stenk.

The bwoy sits down in front of me and opens a beige file with just a few pages of paper and takes out his biro pen, cheap and nasty, nothing special there. No taste nor culture, in evidence in this police station.

'Good morning. My name is Chief Inspector Pendlebury.' The bwoy gades me strangely. I could almost be thinking at this moment in time he is expecting me to admit I carried out a robbery, burglary, hit and run or even a brutal murder.

I look around the room and as it is all white walls and nothing to see I quickly look back at this important Inspector. He quotes my non. I say, 'yes, that is me, sir.' I decide to give him some respect, starting off very correctly. This approach should go down very well for me now and in the long run.

He nods. He writes something down, probably my non and today's date. He looks straight at me. He looks serious. All part of the act, I am sure.

'You are here today to answer some questions about a death in Coventry and we suspect a murder.'

'I know.'

'Good. You have clearly seen our announcement in the media.'

'Yes.'

'I shall read you your rights and set out our standard procedures.'

'Yes.' This takes a few minutes and he reads it so vitly I can not understand a word he says. It all sounds very sensible and plausible, though.

'Do you agree?'

'Yes.' He ticks the box on my form saying 'advised of rights', I could see as I could just about read upside down. By now, we seemed to have gotten the protocols out of the way and the frightful suspense is killing me.

'Now, I would like to introduce you to someone who is present at the time.'

What, I was very facht by now. Is this awful inhumane monster Bridgen going to come in the room and talk to me? Inspector Bridgen visiting little old me, your Respectful Raconteur. Sisters, where are my useless brothers when I need them, this scares me. Pat and Mom, I forgive you, I zord myself say in my tet. This whole episode is taking a turn for the worse. I do not want to meet Bridgen. I really do not want to meet Bridgen, is this some sort of set up. I shake and cannot control it.

I am sitting here starting to think to myself these feds club together. A very tight bunch once you start to cross their lines. Poor old Sally knew one of her best clients was a jake, yet totally unaware of his past and history. Like any profession, doctors, accountants, lawyers and especially the law, you cannot compromise any of them. They stick together like glue. To me, the fact Bridgen killed my friend then in my view he is perfectly capable of killing me. He could give me a right good going over. A proper batay as some of the past badmen would say with all their bloods.

Would this smug frekan chief sitting in front of me allow this to happen? He is looking at me for my reaction. A donut five-o. Me stuck in this room, in the police station all helpless with this great chunk of patat.

'When?' I question.

'Soon, they have not arrived yet, being ferried down from the Midlands, due at 10.30am.'

I look at my fone 10.00am, a further thirty minutes to wait. Why bring me in at 9.00am, so disorganized.

'In the meantime I shall leave you alone to think.' The cheek of the stoodge. I know my rights. I read up on the winternet over-night. Perhaps I can ask for a rev, if they have one, these days. Possibly not, cutting back due to government austerity. They may not have the budget for any revs these days, just obnoxious young fed recruits. People should pay their taxes. If there is a rev around, I can then ask if he or she can be with me while the mon-ster Bridgen questions me or tries it on, even. A sexual predator. Perhaps he will want to attack me, some banging before he ends my simple lavi. Just like Sally. I am thinking the worst.

The great Inspector gets up and leaves. He shuts the door abruptly and I could see a five-o gal standing outside. I could ask her for a rev.

I open the door. She takes her baton out and with it hits the frame of the door very hard. I reel back but still manage some words.

'No, madam. They are busy today.' I take that as five-o speak they did not exist these days. 'I suggest you sit down and wait for your visitor.'

I must tell you now, yours candidly wanted to be home in my room, the safety and warmth of my four walls. I could give a lot to look at my Dali clock and the cherished silver-frame at this instant.

I am sitting here patiently waiting for the chief to reappear and then five minutes early at 10.25am the door opens.

'Come this way madam, please.' A little pleasantry which is nice to zor.

I walk along a few corridors with the Chief. The corridors are ordained with the most urbane prints and pictures of the local area. The authorities are trying to make it look soft and pleasant but the stenk of authority and jakes abound. Then we enter a room. There are rows and rows of desks with two chairs either end. The desks have a plastic see-through shield fitted along the middle to separate the two people sitting at the desks. This stops those sitting from touching or passing things between them, such as browns or weed. This must be the visiting room. A quick look around and again the white walls are bare, no pictures, no windows and all very very boring.

The Chief stays by my side, which gives me some small amount of comfort as Bridgen could not take me on while he was here, surely. Of course, they may want to have a bann bang, but hopefully not on government premises.

Then the door on the other side of the room to where we had entered, opens.

I cannot not believe my zyes. A chick fed enters and behind her, in walks Sally. My bestie.

You could knock me down with a feather. My grizzle is wide open. Sally looks at me. She is very bedraggled. It looks to me as if she has had no dodo for a few days. Her cheve is a mess and her zyes bleary with black bags underneath.

'Sorry.' Is all she says. She looks so sad. She is not the vibrant, highly amusing and lively girl I knew and wanted so badly as a business partner.

'Sorry for what my darling bestie, is it Sally?' Is the only reply I can muster. I am just so pleased to see her. I am astonished.

'Sorry I killed him. It was your idea and with the screwdriver.'

'What?'

'I got carried away with your ideas.'

At this point in time, the one and only Chief Inspector Pendlebury interrupts. 'Sally, you admit killing Inspector Bridgen and Henrietta here was an accomplice.'

I wait for Sally's answer.

Sisters, as you know I had been nowhere near her on that fateful night. I have never met Inspector Bridgen. I have no intention of murdering anyone, anywhere nor anytime, even though so many stoodges annoy me. Especially these dreadful jakes, particularly the ones I have met only yesterday and today.

Then Sally speaks softly with gravitas. 'Yes, I did do it and she is my accomplice. This is her.'

'In that case,' and the Chief Inspector turns to me. 'I am arresting you on suspicion of being an accomplice to the murder of Inspector Bridgen.' I knew the jakes stuck together like glue, but why me? Why be so hateful? This took the biscuit as Pat and Mom would say. Sisters, this really takes the biscuit.

I look at Sally and she turns her gaze away from me. The gal fed grabs her by the arm and marches her away back out of the room from where they had come.

I was a simple defans to help Sally that night. I wanted more time to talk with her. As I gather my thoughts she is gone. Led away by the fed chick to oblivion.

And my sisters, this is the story how yours candidly is moved out for being an associate in a murder I did not commit nor aid, having not met the victim, having no motive to carry it out and not being within one hundred miles of the area where it took place.

On reflection, I was surprised they had let me stay in my own yard last night. I can only presume they knew I was only going to be an accomplice and hopefully no physical threat.

The more I was kept in the dark and the less I knew then the better. It had been made obvious to me I was going to identify Sally's body.

I may never see Sally again. I feel totoy.

2

Back in my small room at the station I take one of the seats by the desk and sit down. Chief Inspector Pendlebury enters shortly after me.

'There,' he starts, 'Henrietta, you can see she is admitting her crime. And associating you as the person who incited,' he pauses 'rather encouraged her to carry it out.'

Sisters, it is making complete sense now why I am here. He is looking at me straight in the zye. I return the compliment.

'Are you going to charge me, then?' I ask as confidently as I can, in this occasion of high tension.

'If you do not admit your crime, yes. If you admit your crime, then we take statements and continue with the process. Do you admit it? Guilty or not guilty. Just wait a minute I need a witness.' He opens the door and the five-o gal who banged the door with her baton only thirty minutes ago comes in after Pendlebury's request.

'Witness this please, PC Burley.' He turns to me. 'Over to you.'

'Not guilty.'

I come over all efreye inside despite showing a strong exterior with my simple words. I wonder if these two words will mean I get some aggie. I look at the chief and think it highly likely. He grimaces at me, a very unpleasant expression on his grizzle and I stiffen up in readiness.

'Well indeed, quite a stance, Henrietta. We cannot charge you yet, we prefer an admission. We have the messages you sent this girl Sally on her fone, the Whats App notes. Here they are.' And the front of it, he leans across the desk and shows me his fone. His aftershave is stronger and a lot worse now, he must have given himself a booster spray. I feel really totoy.

I read. 'Murder him boom.' This is the first one and the other 'Hope you left him finished. Wapp me when you can.' And finally. 'Do not forget the sharp screwdriver.'

Pendlebury continues with such a condescending attitude, 'I am unclear what boom means, some of your adolescent street talk, no doubt.'

'I can translate for you.' I let him wait for a second. 'Boom means good.'

'There you are then, incitement to murder, it cannot be clearer or more obvious. Young, dear and innocent Sally complied with your wishes. Our very own Inspector Bridgen stabbed to death by a pointed and sharpened screwdriver.'

I can tell at this very moment the chief stirrer here, sitting in front of me wants to protect the rabble they call law enforcement officers and then make examples of anyone transgressing or hurting them. He wants to make sure they can do what they want, when they want, to whom they want. The fact their very own is murdered and probably deserved it, in my view, knowing Sally as I do, then what hope do I have. I feel as useless as my eediat brothers and all those associates who get taken in and accused of all sorts of spurious crimes and tings. I will be treated just like any general 'poor run of the mill' badman. The boys in blue are closing ranks, that is obvious. Sadly, I think they always do.

'Henrietta, we understand you are quite a wizard on the computers. What do you do?' A change of tack and questioning by the chief.

'I am an influencer, selling product and taking a small margin from the product sold.'

'An influencer. You certainly influenced our Sally here then, didn't you?' Chief Inspector Pendlebury says in a sarka tone. Sitting there in his finest suit he sits smugly and turns to the fig chick and fed PC Burley. They smile together. 'I think Henrietta cannot deny the charges, now.' They clearly think they have yours candidly by the bubbles, if I had any, that is.

He turns to me yet again and condescendingly utters, 'how do you plead now, miss influencer, miss supporter?' Not only the tone but also his voice begin to grate with me. To the extent I only have one answer and two words to say to him, again.

'Not guilty.'

I wanted to say so much more but hold my ground. How could yours candidly start to admit to a crime when I was physically nowhere near it. The world is mad and fast getting worse with the likes of Bridgen, Pendlebury and Burley roaming the streets in their fast cars and shiny glarbies. I am physically sick. 'A bucket please,' I manage to say just in time as the fig little chick hands me the wastepaper basket and I immediately send some totoy into it. What a stenk in the room now. My totoy and his aftershave. Chief is forced to open the door for fresher air. PC Burley takes the bucket and sprays some air freshener. She becomes somewhat useful, after all.

I feel better and gather myself and my thoughts.

Sally must have had good reason to deal with Bridgen the way she did, surely this is our answer and the way out of this mess. A mess to which I seem to be innocently and inadvertently involved. It is nearing lunchtime and I have not seen a moun to identify yet. Quite a change of events to what I was expecting when I entered this godforsaken place, earlier this morning. But I am not at all comfortable with the way the events are turning, as pleased as I am to see Sally, alive.

But her statements are making me complicit and her actions rub with me and rub badly. Why is she doing this. Perhaps she is forced to?

'This wonderful Inspector Bridgen of yours, what happened to him and what is his track record?' I decide to take the initiative.

'What's it got to do with you?' Pendlebury answers aggressively.

'Everything, if you are accusing me of being associated with his murder.'

'Geoff Bridgen had been in the force about thirty years and was well respected by his peers. He was currently taking a six-month sabbatical having worked extremely hard and long hours over a period of three years investigating and prosecuting a child trafficking ring in the Midlands, involving child prostitution. A model police officer. In fact, a role model to us all.'

Yours candidly cannot believe her zoreys. 'What?'

'Yes, a wonderful career and a leader in his field and destined for promotion and beyond. Could well have become the Commander of the Midlands force with the trajectory of his career.' The chief looks down at the floor very melancholy and grief stricken. 'Struck down.'

'What?' I need confirmation of this obituary. 'How did he die, then?'

'Your friend, this girl Sally, met him one night on the pretext of giving him evidence. We have it well documented in Geoff's diary and taped messages on his fone and work desk fone. She lured him and then stabbed him repeatedly with this screwdriver weapon, the very same which you, young lady, encouraged and influenced her to take to the meeting.' He chooses his words carefully.

'I merely mentioned the screwdriver as a method of self-defense.' Downplaying the need for the murder weapon and changing subject. 'Sally is such a small thing. How could she overpower him?'

'She stabbed his eyes out first.' Clever girl, his zyes first, I could not help thinking. 'Then once he was incapacitated and struggling to know his bearings she took his wrists and stabbed there, and he just bled to death in the ditch into which he then fell. She even taped his mouth so he could not make any sounds or cries for help.'

'Quite a good job.' Pendlebury's description warrants my comment. A comment full of insolence from their viewpoint but full of praise if you take Sally's side. As I do.

'You could say that. But we think she is put up to it and in the pay of the gang who Geoff put down. Do you know any of these names?' He shows me a list, none of which I recognize, the nons some being all foreign and that. 'We shall need to download your computer to see the emails you have been making these last few weeks, miss influencer.' His sarka tone is very annoying.

Not if I can help it and I need to get there first. I then panse about the winternet report I read about Geoff Bridgen. Attacking another female officer. Is this not true?

'I thought Inspector Bridgen,' well done Henrietta some respect calling him his official non and leaving this 'Geoff stuff' to the rabble in front of me, 'was off work because of some indiscretions at the very same workplace.'

'You have read the internet report, you knew Sally was going to meet him then.'

Caught again, by this not so bumbling Chief Inspector. 'Yes, I did know this fact and can tell you why I know, if you want to know?' Stand firm H.

Pendlebury continues. 'Geoff allowed that to happen to entice the transgressors to believe he was not on to them, lead them on, you see.' I panse not a good enough reason for yours candidly. He carries on digging this great big hole. 'Don't read everything you see on the internet as being the gospel truth.' Kind words and advice for me considering I, yours candidly the Respectful Raconteur, am the hacker in chief of all world-wide hackers.

'I don't.' Even though I put a lot of this deception on the winternet myself.

'Good for you. So poor Geoff was stricken down by this girl Sally. Why do you know this, were you trolling him, are you part or know of this child trafficking gang?'

It is time to bear all to this Chief Inspector about everything I know. Then to see what he makes of it all. I am thinking to myself I must not lose sight of my objective and my end jwet, which is just to get home in one piece.

'Look Chief Inspector Pendlebury, I met Sally at university. She became a good friend. She struggled financially and often met men for sex, paid sex, to get herself through. To allow her some safety she gave me the details of the men, or as much as she knew, such as names, addresses, phone numbers, emails and credit card details if the punters did not pay cash. It could be said I was her guardian angel. That is all there is to it, really.'

Pendlebury does not appear phased with this information. 'Did you ever meet any of these men?'

'No.'

'Why then, did you troll Geoff Bridgen?'

'A couple of nights ago, she mentioned she was meeting him. So, even though I was busy with my influencing and internet business, I look him up and read what there is on the internet. This is all there is to it.'

'What are you implying?'

'Inspector Bridgen was put to me as being her client,' I added, 'just one of the many.'

'Is this what Sally said? Interesting. I think we need to

interview her again and then come back to you. Under the Human Rights Act and as you are an accomplice in this crime, we are going to keep you in overnight. I suggest you speak to your family. Please use your fone.'

'If I am to stay here, then I need my kompyuter. I can call my brother?' I ask. For the first time ever, I will ask him for assistance.

'Yes, you can have your computer we shall be here to collect a download. We cannot deny you access to your phone or computers, because at this juncture in proceedings we have not charged you and you have not admitted the crime. We want you to admit this crime of all crimes. You can see our motivation, though.'

'I need proof of this gang.'

'Once you admit this crime, we can tell you everything. Admission will be easier in the long run and there will be plenty of time for all these statements and disclosures. But,' he pauses, 'now I do believe you need some help.'

Yours candidly wonders what he means by those words, 'need some help'. It must certainly mean a good criminal lawyer, provided by the state, despite cutbacks, to help yours candidly while I am in this unholy mess. Helping Sally had meant I did not help myself. She does not deserve any of my dosh or assistance she can go from here on her own from now on, as far as I am concerned. No business partnership in the offing for you, young lady. A Digital Tomato will have to stay at Web 2.0. No augmented reality, no cryptomatoes and no metaverse. I did not like being treated nor spoken to like this. I am getting angry at the pesky attitude from the jakes.

'We shall go round and get the kompyuter shortly.' PC Burley says. I do not like this fig chick fed one iota.

Both jakes leave me. Why do they want to get my kompyuter here? Surely, they are slow on this one, I panse to myself. I need a replacement for home as I shall lose this forever. Anyway, less thinking and planning and more doing. I pick up the fone.

'Cyril, thank goodness you replied.' He normally let it go to answerfone but the intrigue of my welfare, once he saw it was me calling, probably got the better of him on this occasion.

'I saw it was you, sis. Are you OK?'

'Not really, still here. OK, enough of that, I need you to get me a new kompyuter and fast. This is for home when I get back later.'

'You going to come home soon, then?'

'Not just yet. But here are my credit card details.' I blurt out my sixteen-digit number card details and the PIN number. There was a £15,000 credit limit on this card and no balance at all, always paid off each month. I then gave Cyril details of the kompyuter I need.

'The fig chick PC Burley will be along soon to collect the original. Now listen. I need to download everything from the current kompyuter to my fone which I have here, and to do it now. Can you go into my room?'

'Such trust, sis.' I could tell Cyril felt lifted by this new respect and responsibility.

'No time for being sarka, I am in trouble, say nothing to Pat and Mom, yet. Please. Here are the details of how to download and send.'

I know Cyril can do this perfectly adequately. This is something those apes can do, manage simple kompyuter instructions. Why they both did not take it further is beyond me? Lazy imps. However, they are being useful now. I must not complain.

I look at my fone and there is sufficient signal. The download is working. Good old Cyril.

'It's finished, are you still there?'

'I am, sis, what next? Can I come and see you?'

'Yes, for sure, you can come back with them into the police station when they go home to collect my kompyuter.'

'Great fun, what an adventure. And Albie?'

'No, just you.' I make myself very clear on this one.

'He won't like that.'

'Well, stuff him. One last instruction, Cyril. Switch the control panel to B.'

'Done it. See you soon.'

I have my kompyuter in front of me and on Master mode I can now see where I am with A Digital Tomato and any messages. I can also remotely delete files from the kompyuter in my bedroom on B. I have the control here in front of me. I feel normal for the first time this morning. I settle as I am back in control mentally. My digital world surrounds me but physically I am completely in the wrong place.

Then there is a knock at my door of this godforsaken little room.

There in front of me is a fraff dressed, elderly woman, about ansyen. 'I am Miss Chambers. The therapist assigned to your case.'

The last person I want to talk to now, just as I now have my most precious tool in my hand. The authorities send in a stupid, time-wasting and unnecessary, probably also extremely costly, therapist.

No sign of a proper rev, just a therapist.

No sign of doctors or men in white coats or my bestie, just a therapist.

The revs and doctors and their like may still be lurking somewhere in the depths of this hell hole, though probably just about to appear.

And most importantly no sign of any escape back to my parans' yard.

3

Miss Chambers enters my room as I am sitting here waiting to do other much more important things. She sits opposite me. She looks to be quite a force. She reminds me of the fearsome headmistress who performed daily at morning assembly at my primary school, all those years ago. Very bossy, nosey and totally uncaring, in fact impudent. Exactly the three traits I do not like in people. The type of person I take a distinct and immediate dislike towards. Bossy, because she is always right, nosey because she asks awkward and personal questions and impudent because she does not seem to care if she crosses the line. She will have some chutzpah, for certain. I look at her, if not stare and she stares back. She looks at her file and opens it. There is a list of questions, I can see this much. She takes out her glasses for her zyes and they are those really plum ones, the small, little and ineffectual pince-nez. My word, with those she looks even more stupid than before. Her hair is short and tied in a bun. She has wrinkles and I panse she is about sixty years old. Older than Pat and Mom, in my judgement. A small mouth and smaller nose. They do not seem to fit the fig face that presents itself in front of me. Or perhaps the large fig and red mug just make the nose and mouth smaller. Her choice of clothing is even worse. For a top she has a yellow blouse covering her buxom tetes. On that she is wearing a mauve cardigan. They clash. Someone should tell her. Then a brown skirt completely incorrectly setting off the ensemble on her upper half. Her stockings were the non-see through type, the type only frumpy women wear, and her black soulyes look like sandals on her janms. All entirely unfitting and really quite ugly. She looks at me as if she is going to start to talk and then refrains. What is wrong with the woman, am I supposed to say hello and welcome her to my world? Surely not, after all she is the therapist. What joy I am going to have. I will have fun, believe me. She opens her mouth again and words are uttered.

'I am Miss Chambers. The therapist assigned to your case.' She repeats.

'You said those words as you came into my room.' I decide to exercise a territorial right to my humble, yet temporary, abode within the police station. After all I have been here for two hours already today. This room is mine.

'Well, it is polite to introduce oneself and allow the chance for you to know me, my name and purpose.' Miss Chambers comes back with an eskiz, my word, I am winning. 'Your name is Henrietta?'

I confirm and recite all my names. She writes them all down. 'How can I help you?' I ask her.

'It has been put to me by the authorities they are recognizing abnormal behaviour in your personality and wish it to be analysed before they take any further action. This is because a programme of assistance will be better for you the patient and also so much fairer by far,' then she needlessly adds for effect, 'less costly in the long run, for the state.'

'Can you repeat this please?' She does just that. I understand I am now a patient and the state wants to save dosh on me. Bully for them, what a lovely state authority. Control in my view, a totalitarian state. Authoritarian, oppressive and tyrannical, it all seems to me plainly set out in front of me, oh, sisters. First charged with murder and now being assisted due to my alleged personality disorder, can it get worse?

'To help me analyse you, it has been noticed and not by me, as we have only just met,' full of eskiz she maintains painfully, 'that you possess behaviour which can only be described as unlikely to be considered the norm.' She completes her mini lecture with a knowing look. As if by chance I were to accept this diagnosis. What is the norm? I panse.

'Give me an example?' My challenge is required right now and delivered.

'You work alone in your room all day long, hardly venture out and do not seek the company of other humans.'

'A loner,' I summarise for her.

'In one word, yes. We can correct this by one of the primary goals of counselling and training therapy. The first item to achieve is to make you become self-aware of this trait. Clearly some people with a trait such as this have little insight or depth into their own problems.'

'I choose not to mix.' My emphasis is on the word choose.

'Miss Chambers, it is my choice.' I repeat the simplicity and clarity for her.

Ignoring me she continues, 'all these people seem delusional. It occurs because many of us have an exaggerated sense of the uniqueness of some private, non-shared, even perhaps *forbidden or disapproved of* thoughts or behaviours. All of us, Henrietta, and we will come back to your name, hide aspects and certain elements of ourselves and can suddenly see these alluded to in books, papers or manuscripts which list all types and sorts of abnormal behaviour.'

'What are you saying?'

'You are a private person. The real Henrietta is not out there yet. You need to be able to express yourself more and perhaps join a peer group to discuss these things.'

This is fascinating stuff, she has a point, but I have not met any mouns to whom I wish to open up and declare my inner panses. She put it eloquently, in fact bluntly, my sisters, yet very vividly and with good expression. This will be fun.

'I like your colour of hair, the yellow is striking. What is your natural colour?'

'Boring black.'

'There you go, you need to strike out from the abnormal back to the norm. The problems with abnormality and any such definition are firstly a healthy person in an unhealthy society can be labelled as such.' This is me for sure. She is making sense and continues, as she acknowledges I am taking it all in. 'There are many examples of societies which have been so very deeply intolerant of those who do not follow narrow standards of belief and behaviour.' She introduces religion into this by using the word belief, I was just pansing it will follow on soon and become a natural fallback position for her. 'Secondly, experts cannot agree on the categorization of normal behaviour contrasted to abnormal behaviour. Statistics produce norms but then you need to review the outliers. This gets harder as the scope of the selection increases. Outliers are created for a variety of reasons.' Miss Chambers is starting to make excuses for her work. This will be a win win for your Respectful Raconteur.

'I understand. But being a loner is not a crime. It means I keep myself to myself and do not bother others.'

'Very true, Henrietta. However, culture dictates we mix as humans and seek company. You do not. This is abnormal.'

'Throwing normal cultural behaviour at me is not washing with me.' I disagree for the first time. I gade at her. I cannot screetch.

There was a knock at the door and there stands Cyril, thinner than ever all awkward and everything. Miss Chambers looks extremely annoyed at being disturbed. I like that. He put her off her procedural plan of attack on me.

'Sis, your kompyuter.'

'Thanks, Cyril, thanks so much. Have you transferred the data to the other new kompyuter?'

'Yes, of course. All done. The officer at the front desk wanted this for five minutes, that is why I am a bit late. A letter for you, too.'

'Great news. Strange a letter. I am busy with Miss Chambers, she is helping me.'

'OK, leave you to it. Mum and Dad send their best. See you later.' I liked Cyril's style, it is all hopeful and I knew I shall be away from this godforsaken place soon. As he leaves, I wink at him.

'Your brother?'

'Yes, as stupid and as dumb as hell, but he cannot help it.'

'You seem frustrated with him.'

'Yes. And his brother.'

'You have two brothers? That is not on your notes.'

'Twins.'

'I need to correct this. Let me just write this down, they are younger and live at home.'

'Yes. They have persuaded my parents I should leave home and give over my nice comfortable and safe room to one of them.'

'You resent this?'

'Wouldn't you.' I pause. 'Of course, I do.'

'Another criterion for abnormal behaviour is poor adaptation. Not being able to do the everyday things of life, such as hold down a job, you don't. Maintain happy interpersonal relationships, you don't. Plan for the future, you don't.' There is a silence. 'And clearly resent all of this as well.'

The granfem is making sense and almost making me believe my own shortcomings. How dare she take this line with your Respectful Raconteur?

'Your name. Inspector Pendlebury wrote down a number of names, you use. Not only, Henrietta, Enrietta, Etta, Henri,

Henry, Hal and perhaps even H. Amongst others. Why? A crisis with identity?' Miss Chambers looks at me inquisitively.

'I choose the name that fits the role I am doing that day, but my real name is Henrietta.'

'A crisis of identity is where individuals look at themselves differently in variable settings.'

'I do. Henrietta today for the formal piece. Etta for my game development days and perhaps other names for the varieties of activity. This is normal?' I turn the situation around.

'No, it is not normal behaviour. You have one name, given at birth.'

'Some change it by deed poll.'

'They can go through that lengthy and legal process.'

'But my various names are only derivatives of the main name, so that is normal.' I decide to argue. I want to extend this argument further but I can tell Miss Chambers is becoming freekan with her superior knowledge and all that. I blodclot. 'It's all so bloody stupid. This whole affair.'

Then it all kicks off.

'Do you plead guilty or not guilty?'

'Not guilty.'

I continue when I feel Miss Chambers has digested the two words. 'It's about time this stupid woman, Sally, backs off my case. I was helping her that awful and fateful night and this is the reward, innit?'

She writes this down on my notes. I enjoy being on my sel, what has it got to do with the damn authorities. Trying to make a problem out of nothing. I could tell the woman sitting in front of me would be forthright and try to ask the awkward questions. To date, I think I have done well, but she could well grind me down, that is, if I let her.

I open my fone. An email from Gio. 'What the hell does this bloke want now? I have told him to sling his hook.' I say afo.

I read to myself. 'Digital Master. I have created a protest group against you. You will be hearing from our lawyers. Giovanni New York.' Then I say afo, 'the idiot, what a waster.' Miss Chambers looks at me aghast.

Cyril had passes me a letter. It was a brown envelope and all official looking. I open it and say, 'they put this sort of thing on such kaka, shit, paper, don't they?' Miss Chambers looks at me disdainfully. 'What the hell does this woman want now?' I almost shout.

On reading it quickly, it seems they do not accept my excuse of winning at Newbury. Surely, they, the tax authorities, have done the mathematics, it all works out.

'Another fight to fight, the damn taxman all over me.' And on this occasion Miss Chambers stands up and away from the table, just as I spark the table and it makes quite a noise. Her file lifted about an inch and falls back down. Miss Chambers looks startled. I chort to myself.

Then there is a ping on my mobile fone. 'What's this about?' I search for my fone in my bag and pull it out. 'My credit card maxed out. The dillbats, my brothers spending my damn dosh. The losers those two. I tell you. They have got a lot to answer for.' My larenks is getting foer and foer. 'And now just as they had my card number and I give them the PIN and they spend all my credit card balance. Absolutely pathetic the pair of them, you just saw chief loser himself,' I look at Chambers, 'and his brother is no better.' I stare at her and after a few seconds I add, 'in fact much so much worse. Fancy living with them?'

'Look, Henrietta, I shall leave you to settle down and will get some more help for you.'

'Thank you, may I have a glass of water and a sandwich, I think it must be lunchtime.' My voice is cotched, for the first time for a while.'Yes, of course. I shall write up my notes and make further recommendations.' And with that Miss Chambers leaves the room and yours candidly to herself. She stumbles in her rush to the door. A win for young Etta.

The meeting passed very quickly. Her therapy and purported help did not last long. Or is it me and my reaction to everything? Perhaps she has a point. It may be me with all the self-doubt and all that is going on around me.

I am pleased to be alone, I gather myself. The audacity of the woman to say I was abnormal. The brass neck of the authorities to have me here as a dunfa. I must admit, I find the effrontery of holing up this good-natured taxpayer, appalling.

I sit there wondering what will happen next as the little, fig, fed, chick PC Burley appears with a glass of water, some crisps, a yoghurt and a sandwich.

'Nice, cool. Thank you.' She just smiles as if she knew something I did not.

Some time to myself on my sel and a look at the kompyuter which Cyril has brought me. The chance to erase some files and read emails.

A time to reflect. I panse of Sally. Why is she implicating me in this whole mess?

4   I panse to myself the details on the track records of all Sally's clients may help my case. However, I take the view, due to the observed abnormalities of my behaviour witnessed by the authorities as a loner, I should play them at their own jwet. Also, the clients, with all their nons and addresses, are either innocent punters or are the actual child trafficking ring themselves. 'Good.' I say to myself. 'The files about Sally and all her goings and comings are now erased. The least I know about her or have anything recorded on my files, the better.' The less I am involved it must help me. I could get wrapped up into something which does not interest nor concern me. Such as this child trafficking ring, which actually disgusts me and should disgust any normal person.

    I am not abnormal. As I said before in this dosye, I am not punk.

    The way these jakes are hovering over me with all their control, fear and bullying tactics the worse it could get for yours candidly. I do not seek to escape but I know I can talk my way out of this. I just need some more time.

It is getting quite cold in here.

Then I decide to read the letter from Mrs Dharsanny, the taxman. This is such a quick reply from my letter sent only on Thursday. I see it is sent first class and her reply is the very next day. They must be working hard in her office and sparing no dosh. I chortle to myself.

'Dear Madam, thank you for your letter answering my enquiry in respect of the employment or earnings you are achieving. As a result of your reply, as credible as it may seem, I have decided to open a full enquiry into your affairs and would be grateful if you could provide me with full details of all bank accounts you have world-wide as well as the details of the trans- actions behind each credit entry. Please find our booklet on your rights and the need for accuracy and full disclosure in your reply. We can give you 30 days from the date of this letter to answer. Yours etc.'

How really very kind of her. Thirty days, the start of which I am incapacitated in here, this small and extremely bare and very cold room. A few days lost which is not a good start. I eat my meagre lunch, courtesy of the state, by the way.

A credit card maxed out and then Mrs Dharsanny on my back, what a turn of events. Gio talking to solicitors and the girl Sally still making out I am as guilty as her and I had never even met this Geoff fellow. It gets worse. All I want is my room, warm and secure. To look at my Dali melting clocks and glance at and touch the silver-frame, which Gran Betty liked so very much, by the way.

A knock at the door, continued politeness and in walks Chief

Inspector Pendlebury and a younger, fitter woman. She looks as if she could be one of my avatars, as my lespri wanders.

'I need your computer,' the Chief Inspector states firmly. He leans across and takes it. The aftershave stenk waves across me once again. 'Now, we only have to look at the download we made and compare it to these files and we can see what you deleted while on your own. This will give us the important files. Time saver. Clever, eh?' He looks at me for a recognition of his ingenuity. I give none back in return.

The dillbats playing me at my own jwet. This Chief Inspector was something else, and as I sit here, I think he may have done this before, many times in fact. This is my first time in front of the feds and I have already made a few mistakes. Nothing yours candidly cannot recover from, just wait, watch and see. Have faith, sisters. I have the gift of the gab, as they used to say in London and all the street slang to go with it and to back it up.

He turns to the chick and ushers her in. 'Henrietta, let me introduce you to Miss Archer. She is here to help you with more therapy and your anger management. Miss Chambers' report was extremely informative about your condition. Miss Archer, over to you.' She sits down, he walks out and leaves us alone.

I panse to myself. Anger management, what the hell is all this about. Another therapist. Miss Archer is no older than me. She is a brunette and looks a bit dippy to me. One of those do-gooders but she had no idea what she is doing good about nor what is cold and needed protecting. Long brown hair, quite fit thin features and a shapely moun. Small but nice tetes. Her rass is not that cold either. A short enough skirt that it rides up to mid-thigh when she sits down. I saw the chief taking a gazzy. Dark tights and smart high heels. She is dressed in a sort of black and grey throughout, very tastefully put together. Such a contrast from Miss Chambers. Miss Archer wears enough make up to accentuate her features. If I was a bwoy I would fancy her, without any doubt. A bang or a press cross my lespri.

'Henrietta, as Chief Inspector Pendlebury just said, I am Miss Archer and here to help you with your anger management. Miss Chambers made a full report on her findings and said she left you in a state of some anxiety, upset perhaps, flustered and distressed. Very angry with mundane general matters, those which one faces in ordinary normal life, she wrote down here.' Miss Archer reads from the notes in the buff file in front of her.

Why do they keep using the word normal, no-one is normal, after all said and done. 'I am being accused of murder, is that bloody normal?' I say calmly. 'Is that what Miss Chambers reported. She only met me for a few minutes. How do you find me?'

'Well, on the face of it,' she pauses, 'calm, but I do not know what is brewing underneath. Let me explain. Emotions are powerful social signals. Evolution has left us with a set of highly adaptive programmes, all designed to solve specific survival problems, often hailed as coping mechanisms.' Sisters, this is interesting stuff, let's listen. 'We all inherit macro and micro ways of dealing with encounters from past experiences. Fear is the greatest anxiety of all. Fear of being attacked, being wrong, being short of food or water, anything which puts you at great risk. One of six such ways of coping is to show anger. Others are happiness, surprise, sadness, disgust and, of course, fear itself. Anger ordinarily tops this. It is an immediate reaction. You must recognize this?' Miss Archer seeks her first engagement with yours candidly.

'How do I react?' I say, and I panse to myself I might as well learn as much as I can today from this chick. I am not paying for her.

'Not well. First, there is the facial and non-verbal expressions, showing a level of control. Being surprised or shocked leads to a strong reaction, it can lead to a *higher than normal* heart rate, for example. Second, there is the physical awareness of the emotion such as a blushing, but then third there is the verbal diatribe which can often be uttered or follows on by those that lose control. The word control is the key word. If you can control your emotion in this high state of anxiety, you win. If you cannot, then you lose control and possibly commit crimes or perhaps murder or even incite murder. This is why, and the reasons behind why, you are sitting here in front of me.' Miss Archer is full on with her textbook explanations. She must have passed all her examinations with extra credits.

It had not been long for the chick to bring us both back to the matter in hand and why anger management is critical to how the authorities were viewing me and my case.

'Do you realise I have never met this Bridgen person, your good friend?' I add with contempt.

'Not my friend, Henrietta, but sadly my previous and past associate. Who is no more.' She looks at the ground, with a sadness. 'Children pick up all these emotions very early and mainly from their early care providers. We shall have to interview your parents about any particular character traits you had and possessed while young. I am thinking about any distress, crying with your hand in your mouth, anger, screaming and temper tantrums, trying to get what you want and frustrations, such as scratching or teeth grinding or kneading your feet. You may still portray some of the traits. They are often not easy to break. One may not grow out of these as on occasions they do not wear off easily. Some stay long past adolescence and into one's adult years.'

'Interview my parents?' My larenks is firm and raised.

'Yes, later not now. We need to understand you. What is bothering you?'

'Right now.' Well at those words yours candidly decided to let her have it. I raise my larenks. 'Miss Archer this whole charade.' I start. 'I am here under false pretenses.' I pause. 'I am very, very angry. Extremely angry.'

She looks knowingly at me. The chick needed a good good spanking, a bit of aggie would do no harm for her. I could really correlate my thinking with badmen of the past at this very and exact minute in time. I understood their thinking. A few beatings, attacks, murders and a good aggie of some of these useless mouns is the only and right way forward. This chick had mentioned control and she is right, I need to exercise control. It would be far more effective to take control and question her.

I take the route into erotica. As a fit young woman she must have experimented into a lot of different sexual behaviours. Let's try her out.

'Are you happy with your sexuality?'

'I am questioning you. It is not the other way around.' She tries to take control of the interview.

'One simple answer to this question is to answer if you have had implants in your breasts or even your buttocks to try and enhance your sexuality. You are an attractive girl.' The final sentence complimenting her should go far.

'To move on I shall reply. I can see you will not leave this line of questioning. I have not had any implants.'

'Why not?'

'It is not necessary in my view.'

'What about others?'

'I have not asked any others.' She replied vitly.

'Do you have a boyfriend?' I ask, to delve yet deeper into her personal life.

'Just finished with one, but it's not about me, it is all about you.'

'Why did you finish, with him?' I persist.

'He wanted attention all the time. Too much.'

'You didn't fancy that then?'

'No.'

'Ever been with another woman?' I did not try lips with Miss Archer although it may have been quite sensual.

'No.'

'It is fun. I went with Sally at uni once,' I lied to see the chick's reaction. I smile at her and move a hand across the table with an open palm, searching. I am enjoying testing her. Her mug shows she finds this pesky.

'Really?' she questions. 'And I thought we were just starting to get somewhere, after I had set the scene of why I am here. My explanations of your current position were given in full. In summary, I feel you are very disturbed.' A great reaction I had hit a nerve with these earlier comments.

'I don't.' I hold my hand there for her to touch it. She pulls away.

At this she rises from her chair, closes the files on the desk, crushes them into her bag and charges out of the room, nearly knocking PC Burley over in doing so. I could not believe my luck. She did not last long. What a waste of time, gave up so quickly on me and I was just about to have some real fun with her.

The little, fig, fed is still stationed outside my room. A defans for this dunfa yet again.

I look at my fone, no more messages. I give some panse to what I need to do next. Write to the taxman. Compile an email to Gio and sort out my dillbat brothers.

Then without notice old Pendlebury comes into my room, no knock this time. What a lack of respect, I panse.

'Henrietta, you seem to have upset Miss Archer.'

Facht her, little old me, not at all. How could I? 'I said nothing to upset her.'

'She said you started to talk about sexual behaviour and she is here to interview you about anger management.' Well, yours candidly is of the opinion once a therapist always a therapist and they can cover all the subjects on hand. Every addiction, each form of neurosis and all types of personality disorders. I have zord of so many tings: phrenology, aphasia, dyslexia, psychophysics, hallucinations, for starters, then delusions,

the sub-conscious brenn, multiple intelligences, cognitive differences, self-deprecation, selfishness and the rest of the plum
group of mental frigs affecting the brenn. It is all there.

'Not really, it is how she took it. I was not offensive Chief
Inspector,' I say in such a soft, calm and feminine way I think
even he is taken in.

'You are an attractive young lady and with such beautiful
yellow hair.' He could have used the slang word, a tomato.
'OK, I shall let you off this one, but I shall tell you we have found
all the files on Sally and her contacts on your computer. We are
starting to believe you, that you were only there as her guardian.'

'Thank you.' I feel myself cotch.

He leans across and puts a hand on my shoulder. 'A perverted
sort of guardian angel, in some sort of Victorian and Dickensian
way.' A saying I do not understand nor care to quiz further and
just nod to him, but had he just started to come on to me? This
tomato will have none of it.

'Anyway, we have another therapist for you. He will be here
soon.'

Pendlebury leaves and I sit here wondering about the biggest
emotion of all. Fear, yes, those imprisoned before me must have
had a lot of fear facing the brutal physical techniques on offer in
those days. Not happening here and now, just soft pathetic therapists trying to correct me and all they have done so far is take
notes, baulk at the first time I answer back or engage in conversation and they say they are here to help me. Heaven forbid. They
are total fakes. I have thought for some time the boys in blue are
all fakes too.

Everyone has a fear of what they do not know. I was fearful this morning thinking I was coming here to identify little, old Sally. I am fearful now as I will have to sort out the taxman, Gio the internet guru, my eediat sisters, chick Sally, the jakes, my dosh, my impending move and now these damn stupid therapists.

However, yours candidly may be about to get released. I had better not answer back nor be difficult. Help is on its way. A third therapist to take notes. What a chort.

There is a knock at the door. A man appears.

'Hello, I am Mr Croft your sexual behaviourial specialist. I believe you are seeking gender realignment.'

OMG.

<table>
<tr><td>5</td><td>With these words, you could have knocked me over with the proverbial feather. Twice, now, in the space of a few hours. I hold my nerve, though and just sit there, taking it all in.</td></tr>
</table>

He had a definite and noticeable nervous tick with his eyes. The eye lids seemed to flutter a lot. He was one of those who, when they look at you, they talk with their eyes shut half of the time. Most disconcerting. There surely must be a therapist for that type of behaviour? What a strange looking matou? A therapist with eyes half closed.

Mr Croft is wearing a dark blue suit, a white shirt and an orange tie. His cheve is short, crewcut style. No grey in his full head of hair, all brown. He has a very soft complexion as if he used all the products for facial cream which had ever been invented, it even strikes me he does not even shave. His hands are well manicured and long and thin for a man. I would have said he is aged about forty, in between Miss Chambers, the old bat of a granfem and Miss Archer, the very young and extremely flirty therapist chick.

'Very good,' I welcome him to my little abode, 'Mr Croft what can I do for you?'

He stumbles as he sits down, I look under the table to see if he has tripped on anything and I cannot believe my zyes. He is wearing high heeled shoes. They are as red as my own cheve had been the other day. One of them is off his janm and the heel is broken. It is bent and unusable, he would have to limp the very moment he got up from the chair. They were a nice pair of soulyes and certainly a pair yours candidly would wear to a posh night out with a long dress.

I chortle and chortle and chortle. This person in front of me, this man, looked at me extremely hurt by my reaction. I cannot help it.

'Henrietta, this is not the best place to start.'

'I agree.' I can hardly speak. My word, this did lighten up my day and all my dilemmas, issues and problems went into the background for the while, I could not think of anything else but poor Mr Croft and his broken heel. 'I know a good shoe repairer in town.' And with those words I chortle and chortle and chortle again, for at least another few minutes. I look at him as he gathers his papers and begins to write notes. 'I am only trying to help.' I add under a modicum of self-control, but these few words are difficult to dizit him, as well.

I am now able to gather myself. 'Shall we start?' I offer to the damaged goods sitting in front of me. Hang on, high heels, what else is he wearing of a feminine disposition, I wonder? My lespri goes racing for a brief span as he starts to speak sensibly about the matter in hand.

'Henrietta, I understand you have seen the general therapist and then the specific anger management therapist, earlier today.'

'True.'

'Good, so I am here to help you with your sexuality. We believe you need to change your sexual orientation.'

'Do you?' Where the hell can they surmise all this kaka from, I ask myself.

'Yes, it is clear from the answers to Miss Chambers, with all your names, which included Henry, by the way. A clue.' He looks at me inquisitively and incredibly smugly. After a short pause he continues, 'and in particular the answers you gave to Miss Archer who mentions that you explode with anger at the least material event and,' he says quietly, 'what others would say are normal life events,' he returned to normal volume, 'so you are clearly, and I use the phrase with best of intent,' he stutters, 'extremely frustrated.'

I take it all in and pause. Then with my voice nearly at a sho-chan. 'Frustrated at what?'

'Frustrated. Let me leave it at that and I shall explain.'

'Yes, but frustrated with what?' I repeat the question seeking an answer.

'Sexually. And with all life has to throw at you, Henrietta. I am a sexual realignment therapist, to ease your frustrations and to make you into a man. You can become Henry. After all,' and Mr Croft blushes, 'Now I am Stephan and so much happier. I notice from your notes you call yourself Henry from time to time. A clear signal if ever there was one.'

'Or Heinrich?' I chortle and chortle and chortle again. I had Stephan Croft in front of me. Mr Croft, the cross dresser and transgender person is starting to tell me to go the same way, follow the same route and change beyond all recognition. I have to chort again. This time to myself. This person and the situation may be more difficult to play. I must be polite and respectful. Care here Hen, but, oh, my sisters what a chort.

'The state will pay for the whole process. If we can sign you off as being in need.'

'The bloody state will pay for bloody what?' I am very, very angry again and show it. These therapists have driven me into this state of high anxiety. The thought of the recommendation that I should be changing my identity to please the state, the authorities and also some trumped up self-important therapists was totally beyond me.

'We have identified some clear reasons why you should consider this. After all, you are mid-twenties and you have no boyfriends. Apparently, no desire to have children and lack a few, if not many, feminine traits. It appears from Miss Archer's report you like other women.'

'Is all this a crime, then?'

'No. But it clearly shows your sexual orientation. Most women, and attractive ones like you, would be looking for a relationship with a man to settle down.' This sounds just like Pat and Mom. 'Therefore, with no children yet, no little babies to cuddle, nurse and nurture. A very female and feminine desire. The normality of normal. In our view, as sexual orientation and realignment therapists, we are trying to align everyone to their normal behaviour. Realignment is the new solution and one of the best answers to solve any anger management issues.' He explains. 'You also appeared to control Sally. The girl in custody for murder. You were her guardian. She did exactly as you said. It is clear. She met Inspector Bridgen and took the murder weapon under your instruction. The awful and dreaded screwdriver.'

'I see a stitch up, here.'

'Not at all, Henrietta. After all, you just told Miss Archer you had a relationship with Sally. It has all become so clear to us all.'

'It was a joke.'

'A joke while you are in custody and being helped with this expert therapy. How can you joke?'

'Helped. You call this help. You now label all this as expert therapy and I have not asked for any of it. It is nothing but a nosey, impudent and unnecessary intrusion into my life. Yes, I joked.' I look at Mr Croft straight in the zyes.

'Yes.' The person in front of me speaks with confidence. And quietly adds, 'I really do not understand.'

'I don't like being told. I am perfectly happy leading a quiet, singularly private life until all you lot came into it. Butt out, I say.' My san pressure and anxiety are certainly rising to new levels. I can tell.

'Henrietta, I understand your view and natural resistance. I went through it and am still in the process of the transgender realignment. However, from my personal experience I have found it very enlightening. My frustrations have lifted. I am no longer angry or hindered by the sex into which I was born. My career has rocketed, I was just a therapist and now I can explain my personal experiences with this new venture. It is fun.' He continued. 'Look, psychologists have identified between sexual identity and your actual biological sex. Your sex and gender identity, which is not binary, is based on your aware-ness of sex, sex role and being the expectation of how one sex should behave and then lastly, sex-typed behaviour, which is the behaviour culture prescribed and proscribed for your new gender. There are differences throughout life. Listen, in most cultures, males are considered instrumental which means asser-tive, independent and competitive while females are expressive, being co-operative, supportive and sensitive. The healthy outlet for all of this is to recognize what you are and align yourself with this. Then there is the attraction to another sex. We have all sorts of sexuality, perhaps the most liberal and less well known is pan-sexuality which means you are attracted to just the one person whether male or female you may meet rather than the opposite or same sex, in general. A very interesting and absorbing new concept, derived from all the years of research. I must admit for myself I was a woman who liked other women and found my body a restriction.'

'I have heard of cisgender but have no idea what this means.'

'That is, I believe, you find your sex at birth.'

'Exactly. I am there. OK?'

'No, we need to discover more, why so angry?'

At this I stop him right in his tracks and take on the tactic and strategy I had taken with Miss Archer. 'What have you left to do.

I presume you have been on drugs. Anything sewn on?' I chortle again.

'Seriously, the drugs are harmless, they reduce certain things and you grow hair where you hadn't had it before. I feel very funny the day after the treatment, but then it wears off extremely quickly and you can go about your normal life unhindered. I do have trouble remembering which shoes to wear, as you can see. I did have a particular penchant for these red things.'

He seems normal after all. I was starting to find Mr Croft agreeable and take to him. 'Yes, as I say they are a lovely pair of shoes. You must repair them.'

'Thank you. My operation is in two weeks, and I am really looking forward to it. Behold and you are set free. I have lived like this for too long and only want to be set free. I had marginal anger issues and must recommend this treatment to you. I must just take down some details.'

'I refuse.'

'It is voluntary, you know.'

'I refuse.'

'We need to complete your forms and then you can take a view.'

'I refuse. What of those two words, don't you understand?'

'I need to see Chief Inspector Pendlebury.' With this statement Stephan leaves the room. He limps with the broken high heel. What an experience this last thirty minutes has been. He left his file on the desk. With no further invite necessary I turn it around and start to read it. Very little has been written down apart from the details Stephan had mentioned, 'a loner, confused and angry'were the words repeated by all the three so-called therapists.

I finish reading just as Mr Croft reappears with the chief.

Stephan offers Pendlebury the floor to speak.

'If you agree to change sex, you get off the crime.' A stark piece of advice from the chief.

'But I am not guilty. I have not committed a crime. Or am I another one of your statistics?'

'Yes, you can admit to lots of other crimes if you wish to do so. I can prepare a list. Then my statistics will improve by clearing up the large number of crimes, murders and attacks in South London. This would be great. Definite promotion, perhaps we can do a deal, my dear.' A condescending reply and one for me to consider while I am stuck in this crazy small room in this extremely strange place they call a police station. The next steps for me may be drug infusion, under Mr Croft's direction, but I think we have moved on in the last sixty or seventy years in this world to this soft-pedalling therapy. A gentler way and probably one which donnens very little in terms of viable results. However, I recognize I am being compromised.

Where is the sensible Sally when I need her?

We have a stare off, again. The chief wants me to admit to lots of crimes to help him and his dillbat associates, all of which were bent, corrupt and totally out of their depth. Probably could not see a badman if one is presented right in front of them. They just hit the easy targets. Wrongly arrest the good people and bully them into submission.

'Anyway, I thought you said Sally was beginning to advise you I am not involved. Answer me that, Mr Chief Inspector Crap and all your stupid bloody arse-licking therapists.' They both, Chief Inspector Pendlebury and Mr Croft shrug shoulders and look at each other, with a resigned, dismayed and uneasy look between them. With these words, I have certainly confirmed their views of me.

Yes, by now at this point, your Respectful Raconteur has completely lost the plot, with all this kaka.

I let them have it and I panse I would face all the hell they would put my way.

I care as I want to get home, but I cannot put up with all this fraff. They, the authorities could write whatever reports they wanted about me. It did not sousi me at all.

All total BS.

6

The chief looks at me aghast.

'Henrietta, we feel you need some time to think about all of this. Is there anything I can do or get for you while you do this?'

I need to think and think quickly. It comes to me. 'Yes, I would like to talk to Sally.'

'This can be organised.'

'Thank you. In private, please.'

'Not in private. But we can stand back in the room where you see her.' He pauses, 'where you saw her before is large enough to accommodate the space you require.'

'Yes, this is acceptable. I trust it is OK for her as well.'

'I shall check. I shall be back shortly.'

Stephan pipes up. 'Henrietta, please think about the release and freedom you will experience. I shall leave the consent forms with you.'

'Thank you.'

With those comments and my clear plans ahead all formulating so quickly in my tet, which differ from all of their plans or recommendations, the two stooges leave me. I was on my sel. I now have some right proper thinking time.

I put on my headphones provided kindly by Cyril with my kompyuter and listen to the man in black. The man so troubled he disappeared for a while in a cave, wrote and sang beautiful songs and appeared in front of dunfas, giving so much back to society. What a man. What an example.

First, I must deal with the taxman. Mrs Dharsanny has left her email address. 'Dear Mrs Dharsanny, thank you for your letter and I am very disappointed to note the contents. The issue being there are bank accounts to disclose and, of course, details of the winnings as credit entries.' This is not an untruth really and follows on from my previous letter nicely. 'Currently, I am incapacitated but would like to explain one thing. I can direct you to the darknet where there are lots and lots of people earning money. As yet, all undeclared and therefore untaxed, far beyond the amounts you will find from me. There are many people trading on Emarq. They are making huge profits and I am sure this is beyond the reach of Her Majesty's Revenue and Customs, too. I can help, but of course, my request will be you drop all charges or enquiries on me. I await your prompt reply. Yours sincerely,' and all that.

She must bite on this new chargin clever approach. Who would not do so in their right lespri? She could earn far more there on the darknet than from me. It would be far less hassle for me, as well. It is clearly as they say poacher turned jwetkeeper. A great stance Etta, well done. I am careful, though, not to mention A Digital Tomato. Any lead into my activity and fun in my gaming world undoubtedly would mean further in-depth investigation to not only my earnings but also into those honest punters and players who are winning. A Digital Tomato is my fun and play. It is untaxable. In reality, probably not. Anyway, I have batted her back with a good retort and answer. I wonder what she will say next. Send, button pressed.

Now, while I am on my sel, do I deal with Gio or my brothers.

An easy one, dear, little Cyril. Another email.

'Cy, I hope you and Albie are well. Sis here, stuck in this donut police station. I was so very facht and disappointed receiving the message you have spent out all my credit card.' What do I say now, considering the £15,000 is immaterial to me. Do I let him know this or play on his guilt? Playing on his guilt must be the first step to take. 'Clearly this is distressing as I have no other means of supporting myself. I am distraught. If they offer me bail to get out of this hell hole, how do I do it? The credit card was my salvation.' Perfect. He will not know any better.

I need to end the message so he can come back to me with an idea, any idea. He will not have one, it is a question of finding the nerve that will trigger his guilt. 'Let me know your thoughts. You may be able to take the item or items of goods back and get a credit. This may give me enough to pay some bail.' Just a simple suggestion but the twins need such clear guidance and help like this all the time.

Yes, that reads well. Send, button pressed.

Now some thoughts about Gio. I could leave Gio and his New York crony lawyers until such time as I get a writ or something. Anyway, it may be best dealt with by talking to my own lawyer, so I need to find one. This is something I will have to leave and deal with when I leave this place full of kaka.

I can now read my other messages and establish where the punters and players are on A Digital Tomato. All happy chaps, milling around their Levels. I need to push a few players back and down from Section 2 to lower Levels mainly because I have not devised nor designed Section 3 in full yet. It was going to be Sally's job and domain. I think I will mention our proposed partnership to Sally, if and when I see her.

Knock on the door and some more respect held towards yours candidly. It is the fig chick fed PC Burley. 'We are ready to take you to see the perpetrator.' A big word for such a little chick.

'You mean Sally, my friend.'

'You keep friends like her and as they say, you do not need too many enemies.' She chortles a mocking and sarka chort. What a nasty little fig dillbat.

I reply. 'Something has definitely happened to her. Believe me and you are the last person in the world I wish to discuss this with and engage with.' I give her such a disdainful look, sisters, you would all be proud of me.

With that she hits me with her baton across my rass. It does not hurt but I make out it did. Firstly, to think she had won and, secondly, so she saw no reason to do this again. I limp along in front of her always glancing over my shoulder to make sure she is a little way behind me. Enough distance between us so a further strike could not happen. But it suddenly struck me how these dillbats could lash out at any time. When in power, they exercised this fear with only a little piece of bataying and aggie. I would love her to meet a few of my butch friends in a dark alley late at night. Thugs from the past would have made light work of her. What am I thinking about? I am being dragged back into the ways and means of fighting with physical violence. This is where the pungent and sour lowlife so rampant in this police station take you. It is all a mental jwet now in this new digital world.

We pass a few badmen being led this way and that in various mandem. They all look lost and hopeless. The system had beaten them down. Law and order should be renamed lawless and disorder. The feds were marshalling each one two-handed. They gade me as if I was something special and delicate only having the small fig chick as a defans. No handcuffs nor physical restraint.

I will admit to you, my sisters, I am really looking forward to seeing Sally again. I have been doing a lot of thinking and cannot reconcile the fact she has set me up here. I do believe this could be a set up on her. I must ask her straight. I can understand the contact with me acting as her defans when she met Bridgen has been the link. I shall see what occurs and report back to you.

The grey walls echo and resound with the wails and shrieks from all those patronizing this place who have been walking and stalking the corridors. I am unclear where everyone is going and for what purpose. It may be exercise or just the time in the system when they all change cells. I panse it is their exercise routine, but it seems late for this. There seems a lot of people for just a suburban ordinary dreary and regular police station. Or perhaps the jakes have had success and brought in a bann of miscreants. It is a strange sight, late on a Saturday evening. Quite disconcerting. Drunks and gamblers most likely, the public houses get rowdy once the horse racing and football has finished and the working men are either drinking their winnings or drowning their sorrows. What a life, no hope at all. The authorities do not care. These chellos are recycled all the time.

We turn a corner and there is the entrance to the large room the chief mentioned. The fig chick opens the door and beckons for me to sit down. I obey, why not?

I am here alone. The fig chick retires to the back of the room. She is out of earshot. I am waiting for my bestie Sally. I do not have to wait for long.

The door opens at the other entrance and Sally appears with a jake officer loitering behind her and shuts the door. Sally walks to the desk in front of me. Her steps are uncertain, she stumbles. She half smiles at me. It is good she seems to recognize me. Only her, yours candidly and PC fig chick Burley are in the room.

Sally has more scars than she had before, I can tell. She has received some chargin and heavy aggies. Her arms are bruised and spattered with san. She sits. Her face is bruised and her zyes are red and she is sporting a very vacant look. It is as if she is looking straight through me.

'Sally?'

'Yes.'

'It's me Henrietta.'

'Oh, Etta, thank God it's you.' Her voice stutters but her familiarity comforts me.

'You can gazzy me, right?'

'Yes, yes, for sure, but it is a bit hazy. I have just woken up. Something hit me since I saw you this morning and I think I must have passed out.'

'Something?' I question. 'It must have been a fed.'

'Probably, taking their vengeance out on me for what I did to the dillbat Bridgen.'

'You killed him. Yes?'

'Yes, I did.' She pauses, 'he came on to me and started hitting me, he was a brute. The worst I have ever met.'

'So, why did you involve me? Why did Pendlebury here say he was a fine officer? Why did that load of kaka say he was investigating the child trafficking and the frig, all that involves?' I realise as I let out the diatribe, there are too many questions for Sally to answer. I want answers to them all. As well as to all the kaka going on in this police station.

'I don't know I cannot think straight after being knocked out.'

I think to myself she is being beaten into submission and the same time the officers are having their jwet with her while she defends her corner. I immediately think of self-defense. The little, innocent and sweet Sally, who I once knew, would never do this sort of thing.

'OK, one question at a time. Why did Pendlebury here say he was a fine officer?'

'He is not, believe me. The child trafficking ring is complete fiction. It is the police getting nons of young girls who they can play around with. There are no such rings in the Coventry area. Me and my friends at uni have blown this into the open. It is all kept under wraps. That is why Bridgen called me and lured me. Yes, I give men sex for dosh but how else can I get through

143

life and university away from home? My Pat and Mom give me nothing. It is this or the gutter and I want to get on in life, just like you, Etta. Just like you.' She repeats the words and is overcome, she is tearful. I reach across and as I do so PC fig chick hits her baton on the door frame.

'No touching girls.'

'Kaka.' I say. Then I ask, 'why did that load of dillbats say he was investigating the child trafficking and the frig of all that, then?'

'To build a case they were contacting us in the sex industry for police work, not for their own personal satisfaction. They were building their cover, can't you see through this, Etta?'

'So, why did you involve me?'

'Simple. If I was left in here on my own I would just be another statistic. If they took my life as retribution, which they often do, then no-one would be better off or know any more. Human rights are left behind. The other girls are all petrified. The jakes would just get their own way. And all the time in the future, too. They would not let me have any friends or contacts so I decided to involve you. They had my contacts on my fone and, of course, you came up as my last contact and defans. I said you encouraged me, it was the only way I could get to see anyone.' She looks at me wanting. 'I had to. I am so glad I can now talk to you properly.' I feel emotional with Sally's honest explanation. She continues, 'I knew this time would come. I need help. Your help. You need to blow their cover.'

Sally is forthright with her demand. 'OK, why me?'

'Etta, you are mature and sensible and probably the best

144

and most honourable person I know. You can get coverage on this with your winternet connections and all that stuff we learn in university, I know you have taken it on as a business, your messages have told me how excited you are. I can now say to the dillbat Pendlebury you are not involved and he should let you go. Then when the time is right you can blow them away, I repeat, expose their cover'. All the dillbats. Look at me. Will I ever recover.' She pauses. 'They are winning. It is so hard to fight authority.' Her words ring so true.

I feel so guilty. 'Yes, you will recover. This is a good plan.' I give reassurance. 'I am here to help you.'

'Yes, a great plan.' With those words she rises from the desk with difficulty and limps with great trouble out of the room. I am left there alone thinking what I should do next.

We cannot always build the future for our youth, but we can build our youth for the future.

I and my new sister have devised a plan. Can we bring it into fruition and in good time to save all the young girls in Coventry?

While Sally was there in front of me, I forgot to mention my proposal for the new venture which involved her working and developing A Digital Tomato in the metaverse. I knew there would be time to allow me to do this.

Now is certainly not the right time, I panse to myself. Too much else to do.

7

The fig gal fed marches me back to my room, my lovely secure cell. I can only think of my plans and future when I get free. Amazingly, my cell starts to remind of my room at home. I have hope I shall see my haven again soon. Then, reality kicks in. While I have not been charged nor have I pleaded guilty, they are still holding me in custody. Very odd, something sinister in my view. Another charge, perhaps some aggie and a beating, so I surrender to them. It seems to me they still want me to change my identity. The eediat consent forms are still on the table.

A knock at the door, the chief walks in. I think to myself of my immediate release.

'You spoke with Sally, then, eh? What did she say which was new, then?'

'Quite a lot.' I decide to goad him along. To let him think I know more than I should. 'Who beat her up, then?' I ask directly.

'I don't know what you are talking about.' He avoids the pointed question. 'Do you want to be set free?'

'Of course.'

'Then some sex would not go amiss.'

'What?' The direct approach shocks me, even though I could tell it may have been on his agenda from this morning when he put his hand on me. Is Sally right and the bann in the Midlands are really the police? Is Pendlebury one of them? I was sickened with the panse. This stoodge thinking it was his right to come onto me. I reel back from his advance both mentally and physically. The stenk of this creature in front of me, the brazen request, the audacity displaying male dominance so profoundly. I could be totoy right here, right now, again. This is the one occasion during this terrible and most shocking of days when I could offer violence.

Just the thought of being close to Pendlebury who is a frig of a stoodge, drives me to these panses.

'Yes, I do not get it at home. I am always on the lookout for young flesh I can help out. You know the score. Quid pro quo you see. You help me and I, in my position of power, help you.' Blatantly described to me.

'A simple trade.'

'You've understood, so quickly.' His sarka tone makes me so totoy.

'Where?'

'Here. I lock the door and Burley does not come in for thirty minutes.'

'That long?' Pendlebury smiles at my retort. Now my little cell is not like my room at home. The cell could become my living hell. Insecure, unsafe and dangerous.

We are in this awful pause of silence yet again. We stare at each other, for a few seconds and what seems minutes, neither giving ground. He seems to enjoy the power jwet.

Then I say, 'look I would like to see my mum and dad.' Which I hope will bring his temperature and urge right down. It works.

'OK this can be arranged do you wish to call them?'

'Yes, please.' I answer quickly.

With this the chief gives up on me and leaves the room. The awful few minutes pass. I am certain he will be back with more compromises. If the story Sally tells me is true then these officers are all in this for personal gratification, no more no less. All the stories of child trafficking are dreamt up to be their cover. This is awful. I have a civic duty to report this, but who the hell to? Sally and her friends, whom she has left behind in Coventry, are at risk, great risk. If you cannot trust the police force who can you trust? You zor stories of police forces in other countries taking bribes and things and it all seems so unreal and far-fetched but, my sisters, I have just had firsthand experience of it, here, in good old Britain. It is so distasteful. I am shocked to the core.

I gather myself and my worse thoughts pass. I call Pat and Mom. 'Hi, it's me.'

'Darling, are you OK? We have heard nothing from anyone.'

I sound surprised because I am. 'Oh. I have been told by some officials here, and they call them therapists, they have been in touch with you and asking all sorts of questions.'

'No, nothing we would have asked to come and see you. Your father and I have been so worried. We both thought you would be back by lunchtime at the latest. I have a lovely salad here for you, your favourite meal.'

'Thanks Mum, I love you.'

She does not reply at the open declaration of my feelings, because she cannot. She never has. 'The salad is still fresh and here for you.' She turns the conversation around and back to the comfortable subject of the food preparation. Mom is sweet but devoid of any feeling, continually I remain unclear how Pat has lived with her. What do I know?

'Can you come here and see me? I am told I can have visitors, now.'

'Your brother Cyril popped down with the computer.' She corrects me.

'Yes, but he was not allowed to stay, we can spend few minutes together.' My thinking is, if they come here and then Sally absolves me, they can take me home. The initial part of my plan. I need to ensure they will come here. I do not want to spend a night in my cell, the hell hole. Never knowing when the preying stenky vulture Pendlebury may pounce. I just hope he is talking with Sally and being updated with her new statement. His awful aftershave gets stronger every time I see him. What a disgusting human being and holding such a position of authority.

'OK darling, your father and I will come down, he is here nodding furiously. We just want you to be secure. We need to ask you a few questions on money.' Oh my god, that streak of kaka, Cyril has been blurting things out. Possibly bouching all sorts of unnecessary kaka and things.

'Money?'

'Yes, you sent poor little Cyril a nasty message. All about taking goods back and things. What is all this about?'

'Well, Mum, he maxed out my credit card, without any authority or say so from me.' I say in defense of my own reaction being the simple message to Cyril a few hours earlier, which I feel does not need any further explanation, whatsoever, especially to Mom as it is really between Cyril and myself. Cyril is an adult, too.

'We'll be down there, give us a few minutes to get ready. See you soon. We can deal with the money bit when we are all home.'

This is exactly what I want to zor. Some support from my parans just as much as I am supposed to be supporting Sally, my bestie. I panse to myself if I can get out then I can square away with Cyril and possibly organize my affairs such I give him the £15,000. I am sure he would have shared the winnings with Albie, too.

I must take things step by step, very slowly. All matters at this juncture must be directed towards my escape plan from here. Then deal with Sally's requests.

These therapists have been lying all the time, saying they have been taking reports from Pat and Mom. They have not spoken to anyone. This whole dosye is a stitch up. I really do not know how I can uncover all of this. I am unsure if anyone will believe me. I need to think about this. As we all know authorities stick together. I am sure so many before me have discovered all of this, years ago.

My dilemmas and issues have become serious problems now. I am astounded how my simple little life in Surbiton, in my comfortable room has turned completely upside down. My brush with authorities, the police, the taxman and the therapists donnen little help and assistance. They donnen nothing positive, just more and more problems.

I hope Sally is not taking another bit of aggie. I sit thinking of her and then there is a knock at the door.

'Hi, Henrietta.' It is Miss Chambers the granfem who out of the three therapists I liked the most. She seems the one with the most experience and dare I say this, most normal. Whatever normal is?

'Hello.' I may as well be polite. I am unclear what she wants to say to me.

'Well, my dear, we have drawn a blank with your acceptance of any of our up to date and modern therapy treatments.' I sit waiting for her to finish and thinking about past treatments such as aggressive drugs and experiences everyone has been made to sit and endure in the past. 'And also, this is important. Sally has withdrawn her statement you are involved. She has withdrawn the facts you enticed and encouraged her to commit the murder.'

I look at her aghast and a tear runs down my mug.

'What does this mean?' I say in complete disbelief.

'You are free to leave here.'

'Why can't Chief Inspector Pendlebury say this to me. How can I trust you?'

'He is involved interviewing Sally further.'

'Behind locked doors.'

'I believe so.' I read into this she is probably satisfying him and his gratification. I do not condone Sally's actions, I must have and keep my higher standards. 'But he asked me to tell you. I believe your parents are due to arrive.'

'I hope so, I just called them.'

'When they arrive, they will be shown here to collect you.' With this statement Miss Chambers, the ugly little granfem rises and exits my room. It becomes my private domain once more and hopefully not for much longer. I hope this is the last I see of her. To her credit she bustled her way in here to give me the good news. No-one else did that. Like a flash I am, supposedly and allegedly, free. She said so.

I sit all by my sel, but happy. I can leave this place. No more feds in control and no more kaka from the likes of Pendlebury or Burley.

Time passes and I am able to do some deep thinking. I can use the credit card fiasco to my benefit by making sure Cyril and Albie help me from now on. We can become a unit, a real force. Siblings against the world. They will be useful runners if I expand the business. I can always hold the whip over them and make sure they do the right tings all the time. Pat and Mom are not that cold, either. Family is important.

The door opens unexpectedly, the fig chick is standing there, all official.

'We have had word your mother and father are at the front desk. Shall I ask them here or would you like to accompany me there?'

Thinking I don't want them to see my hell hole, I ask to go to the desk to meet up.

The walk takes longer than I thought it would. It seems to be ages going around each corner at a time and then a long straight corridor, I do not remember this at all from this morning. Are we going the wrong way? Or a long way just to prove who is the boss here? A final curtain of control. What dillbats the jakes are.

We arrive at the desk and there they are. All dressed up as if they are going to a wedding or funeral in their own glarbies. I do not need a new credit card for any bail. I am released.

'Hello, dear.' Mom runs towards me and we hug. Pat holds his ground and waits for me.

'Are you OK?' he finally utters.

'Yes fine. Just get me home.' It sounds as if I am imploring them. I am.

We find their car, the smallest ting in the world and all Pat can afford, but I feel protected. The journey is about thirty minutes, slightly slower than earlier. Pat does not drive at break-neck speeds like the five-o. After all, he is used to a larger and unwieldy slow bus.

No one says anything and we arrive home, to the little yard on the other side of town. The front door looks amazing. The plants in the front garden, so tidy. The grass cut in straight lines. Somewhere I can call my home.

I say nothing as I alight the car. I run to the door, find my klef and charge upstairs. My room is as I left it. Just a new kompyuter sitting there. Cyril did well, it looks like an update. I need to reload my files and ensure everything is unscathed and secure.

The nightmare of the police cell is over. My Dali clock tells the time. The silver-framed picture needs a polish. I am relaxed in my very familiar surroundings and it is all I need right now.

Life can return to normal and this, my sisters, is how yours candidly spent a day in the hands of the jakes and learnt an awful lot about life, the authorities and the existence of all the bare faced liars in positions of power.

Liars are everywhere in life. Some even do not know they lie. I shall be on very careful watch from now on. Bed and some kabicha. Deal with everything in the morning.

I had not asked my parans what the televised news conference on the murder had declared earlier the same day. Nor if Pat and Mom had listened to it at all. It had not crossed my lespri, but I am sure they know. This explained their delight at having me home. Cleared of any connection with the murder of such a respected police officer in the Midlands.

The world is fache.

I lie on my bed and fall into a deep dodo very quickly indeed. Screetched.

Part 3

I   'I shall colour my cheve Orange, today. Eh? Orange fingernails and orange toenails. Such a bright colour, but it will make me happy, as I am home. Merky idea, ya get me?'

I feel very good indeed. I slept well for the first time in a few nights and especially after Friday night when I must admit I had an extremely restless swa in anticipation of the day which lay ahead of me. With all the mental exertion yesterday, meeting everyone, three donut therapists, yours candidly, is quite worn out. It is Sunday morning now. The house is very quiet, again. Mom does not work Sundays. Pat does on occasions when his shifts dictate. I am almost certain my brothers have only just arrived home. Messing with cards all night at a frer's house. What a life, they do need my help. For that, I am sure.

While thinking of helping someone, my duty is to my bestie, Sally. I cannot get her immediately out of custody, that is too much to ask. But I could help her by possibly trying to reduce the charges, to manslaughter, not murder, perhaps not going as far as winning her case.

But how? I need to think. It has to be an original thought, as well.

At least, even by only allowing any adjudicator or jury to see another side to the facts presented by the feds. Getting her off the murder charge, perhaps even to manslaughter, must be achievable. I panse I should target a lighter sentence, if it is available, at all, as the first priority. I stream the man in black. I relate to his prison concerts even more now. Seeing Sally beaten up by the jakes, hurt me so much inside. I really wanted to retaliate and give those dillbats a right aggie. They have an awful lot to answer for. They need exposing. If, as Sally says, they are running a child trafficking ring as a pretext in the Midlands for their own rewards. Monetary and otherwise. What questions that raises about all policing in the Midlands area. A right frig. Serious big questions must be asked. And they have to be answered. And soon.

I listen to Johnny Cash playing some soothing music in the background as I lie on my bed thinking. I move on to other artists. I dose. Time passes. I drop down to the kitchen and gather a coffee. It is warm and comforting. Just what I need. Willie Nelson sings 'Always On My Mind', very relevant as I turn to think of Sally's terrible plight. She murdered one of their own. In their eyes, she will pay for it dearly. I feel helpless and consumed by it all.

A sense of guilt then passes over me. Sally drew me in because she knew my actions from the outside could go towards helping her. What can I do? I am in a quandary. I can see her reasoning, tough to take at the outset but entirely sensible and logical for someone placed in her position. They would not have even seen me or ever allowed me in to see her, unless I was implicated. For that fact, I am sure. Sally had played hard, somewhat hurtful but very clever.

I respect all of it. I should expect nothing less from her. She will make a great business partner.

The fed's motivation to see me is clear, another charge, another statistic and potentially another girl to attack. Sickening. If Bridgen attacked her without consent, then she did totally the right ting by stabbing him. In fact, I would have done the same as Sally. Those are the cards you may have to play if you enter that world. Sorry, Sally, you were unlucky in believing the man, who happened to be a five-o, he would play it straight. He didn't. I am convinced many transactions of that nature occur and no harm comes to anyone. Both are gratified, one with sexual pleasure and the other with dosh. A simple deal. On this occasion the result was dramatically different. It should not have been.

Time to think. Time to contemplate my next action. It is Sunday morning. No-one around, so this is the day to scheme and formulate my action plans. Some time on my sel, with just my music. Bliss, immersed in my own far-away siloed world.

I become doubtful and unsure I can help. Yet, it is probable, I can. Then I think of Blaise Pascal's quote. I learned something at university, not just algorithms. Is it likely that probability will lead to certainty. Perhaps not, but I must try. I do not like authority, never have. This is my mission now, not A Digital Tomato and hacking. They may be useful in themselves, they give me the funds, confidence and a network, but my mission is to help Sally. While I think all this through and become highly motivated, I realise I still have no ideas how to help.

However, I do feel very obligated and compelled to do what I can for Sally. If it is not Sally, it could be me or you, my sisters. Today, above all, if you do not go along with the current government or way of thinking you are cancelled or labelled a trouble-maker. It is known as giving out negative speak. Not possible in the past in the non-digital world. Perhaps known simply in those days as cold press.

If I were to win here with Sally, I am likely to suffer greater consequences. I am sticking my neck out against the authorities. This is my biggest challenge yet. The police, the feds, the jakes, all authorities have it in for the ordinary and normal people. In communist countries they call it control. It is here now in Britain, I am very sure of this.

I open my window looking out to the back garden. The leaves flutter in the wind. I bun a brown, it relieves some tension. Tension I did not know I even had. The stenk comes back into the room, but it is comforting.

My proper mission starts here and now.

I lie back and close my eyes. I doze for a short while and it comes to me. The solution hits me in the face just as the stenk of the brown did only moments ago.

I must contact my MP. The member of parliament I did not vote for. I never vote. Perhaps he can help. He may even be implicated in some way as he is in authority but if I can make enough noise and furore he should at least listen. I need to establish who he is and then make contact. An email to him now at this very minute in time. No second to waste. Perhaps, just perhaps he may answer. I need to make it personal. If I do not involve him in this way, then I will most likely be taken as just another crank emailing in.

Who is my MP? I see on the winternet. It is a left-wing chancer. Sir Timothy Adam, who gained his knighthood for services to the state and public service. I conject a complete nonentity. He has been the member of parliament here for fifteen years. So comfortable in his own role and knows the area, hopefully he deals efficiently with his inbox, too. Serving as a junior minister in the Home Office, it looks better to me all the while. He may even have responsibility for the police. No, on further inspection, immigration. Then he is obscurely interested in the settlement and deployment of those who successfully immigrate. Those who are probably being falsely accused of a child trafficking ring in the Midlands.

A carefully worded email may do the trick. Sisters, let us hope so.

He is married with two daughters. It seems they are in the late teens and early twenties. I hypothesize they could be at university, given the life chances on offer to them by his elevated position. They have been born into such a fortuitous family. I take a while to compare them to my own background. I have earned every point on every exam paper myself.

I think Tim Adam will relate to this. I wonder where his daughters are studying. I can hack a few universities and review their admission lists. Anywhere in the Midlands will be a win. If that is the case, I cannot believe my luck. It is turning for sure. As a result, Sally, my dear bestie, you may have some hope, but you do not know it yet. One small step at a time.

Let me think of my email, first. I need to draft it out so it is above all sincere and he surely will have empathy with our situation.

'Sir Timothy. I need to ask for help.' A great start. 'I am a constituent of yours and have been living in your borough all my life. I went to school locally and then gained a first-class honours degree at Coventry University in computer work.' I want to set the scene I am not just some useless crank. I have a worthy background story. 'It has come to my attention there is a child trafficking gang operating in the Midlands. However, it is not as it may seem. The murder of the police officer, you will have seen in the news this last week, was committed by a friend of mine. She is held in custody and needs help. I understand you have daughters of university age and also you are a shadow junior minister for immigration.' Do I add whistle blowing could help his career? Probably not at this stage in this first unsolicited contact. Keep it a straight demand for help. I can add it later should he seem a little negative. I am clearly declaring I believe Sally in this matter not the police officers. Be careful H. 'The trafficking ring is allegedly made up of immigrants to this country, those you encourage, interface with and integrate so capably into society.' A little indulgence. 'If that is the case, you may be responsible for their welfare and well-being.' That is chargin, creating a slant he could be implicated. Well done H. 'I do believe we need a conversation, as Sally while standing there guilty was brutally attacked. It is, of course, her word against the police officers.

Whoever is right she needs a fair trial and to be heard, at least.' Again, an impartial approach. H, you are in such good form. 'I look forward to hearing from you as soon as you can reply. Thank you.' Enough said and I sign off.

My hacking programme finishes. Stacey Adam at Durham University studying French and German, final year, nothing there. But, folks, look wait for it, Alice Adam is at Birmingham University. In her first year studying business and economics.

She is in the critical area, the centre of the hub of all this illegal activity by the police. Young Alice may already have been contacted to help the police with their investigations. She needs to be advised and assisted. I am sure she is not carrying out the same activity as Sally to gain dosh which Sally undertook, but Sally intimated to me innocents are caught up too, compromised and involved as well. The five-o will have the authority, power and strength to call anyone in for an interview. Just look at the brazen sickening approach Pendlebury made on me. The shamelessness of the demand for sex was incredible. Perhaps the report from Miss Archer went ahead of me and he thought I was a nymphomaniac and my needs were rampant and required fulfilling. Whichever or whatever it was, the approach was frig show. The stoodge is a predator and I have every reason to believe the others in the Midlands force are, too. What a horrible mess, sisters.

I re-read my email and add that I know he has a daughter studying in the Midlands. It would not be hard to establish this fact. I see she went to the same school as my brothers, clearly in the A set when Cyril and Albie languished in the F set and even struggled there. The lazy dillbats. If asked, I can mention this obscure relationship. I search Sir Tim's website and there it is, one at Durham and one at Birmingham, it is OK to send. Button pressed, send.

I feel good about this. I wonder what he will think if, and when, he looks at this.

I immediately receive a reply to say he is out of office and will read at the earliest opportunity. Not surprised but it has reached the MP's inbox. At least it went to the right email address.

What else can I do? I cannot contact Sally, but I can discuss finances with Cyril when he wakes. It would be good to get the twins on board with me, establish their guilt yet understanding the need not to nick, at least not from their very own kith and kin. They are nicking from the government, in effect, by being lazy tinedjes. This comes back to the hope and aspiration which is missing so much in their lavis. Actually I do feel for them both.

I listen to more country and western. Gran Betty took long periods listening to Johann Sebastian. I can see the attraction. The beat. The soft background. The ability to escape in the rhythm, for your panses to disappear into a parallel universe. I am lucky I have my warm, secure and private room where I can develop A Digital Tomato. I can programme. I can look out for myself.

I must help Sally, I need to develop a better relationship with Pat and Mom and I think it starts with a good conversation with Cyril and, by default, his ardent follower, the useless Albie. Something wrong with that lad.

As I turn my attention to my eediat brothers, I zor their

door open. I do not want to venture out onto the landing yet. The stenk emanating from their pit will be too strong for quite a while.

I zor steps going downstairs. It is Cyril he always hums the same song. I let him get to the kitchen and I go down and see him there, obtaining a drink of water.

'Cy?'

'Sis, I zord you were home. Great news. Got off the crime then, awful business. A police officer killed. Saw it on the news as well.'

'Yes, I am not implicated, but my good friend is.'

'Best place for her then. Stabbed with a screwdriver. Must have been some struggle. I bet the five-o are giving her a good aggie when they want to.'

'And the rest.'

'What do you mean?'

'Banging, all that business, I think they are subjecting her to a terrible time.'

'Really, that is not right.' Even young Cyril sees the human issues at stake.

'I agree. I have to do something about it.'

'Thought you were going to shout at me about the dosh.'

'I have changed my view on this. While I was held up for the day, I thought why not let you have it, for free, from me.'

'Really?' Cyril is taken aback. He wants to come and hug me, but I pull back from this dubious pleasure.

'What did you buy with it?'

'Do I have to tell you?

'Please. I want to see you have enjoyed it.'

'I shall tell you about Albie first. He put £7,500 into the slot machine arcade at Sandown Park. You know the nice one at the racetrack'

'And?'

'Lost it all in an afternoon, but he says it gave him a thrill. Nothing left. They gave him a nice meal and a few free drinks in return.' Cyril adds attempting to justify his action.

'I bet they did.' I cannot believe my zoreys. I am so stunned the boy had a life chance to go on a course, learn a trade, but no, he went to the slot machine arcade. All lazy, donut and simple like. 'And you?'

'I bought that second hand little mini car, out there. The blue one, here, you can see from here.' He pulls me over to the kitchen window and I can see it parked on the road outside. He seems extremely proud of it. As if his own dosh had purchased it.

'Well done, Cy, good call. An investment, innit?'

'But it costs so much to insure I have no dosh left to be able to drive it.'

Cyril had made an effort but had not thought his actions through properly, at all. These boys need taking under my guidance and wing. They need help. Sally needs help, Pat and Mom need help. Am I the only sensible one here? I shrug my shoulders and go back to my room. Nothing need be said, I had given them the dosh. Cyril will think about it and feel guilty now, no doubt. In his defence, he had tried.

I look at A Digital Tomato messaging board. From Gio.

'Master, my father's law firm are issuing a writ against the per-petrators, and we have crowdfunded the case from the protest group. You will be hearing from us.' A clear and obvious threat.

My luck changes every single instant. 'Total BS,' I panse and then say afo.

Keep strong H.

<table>
<tr><td>**2**</td><td>It is Sunday lunchtime and I know I cannot do much more until I zor from Sir Tim. To be realistic, sisters, I do not hold too much hope out for his help either. I had to try and contact him. I justify this</td></tr>
</table>

much to myself. I try to think of other things I could do. None come to my lespri.

I am wearing my red apparel. It is so comfortable. I feel good. I also have my white kreps on. I have done what I can for now. I look at the silver-framed montage. I touch it and it gives me such strength and great encouragement.

Suddenly a ping. A message. I read it. 'Henrietta, thank you for your email. I have been concerned about the messaging currently being received from Midlands police force. Thank you for your comments about your friend. I am so sorry she finds herself in the predicament she does. The legal processes will take their natural course and I wish the best for her. My own daughter is at Birmingham University and enjoying her course, but as you will appreciate experiencing her first year away from the secure environment of home, she is subject to an awful lot. Perhaps we can talk. Yours sincerely. Sir Timothy.'

I am amazed. I read it all over again. I tingle while reading the content, its politeness and most importantly the promptness.

One piece sticks out to me, '*but as you will appreciate experiencing her first year away from the secure environment of home, she is subject to an awful lot.*' How right and correct he is. He realises, he knows. He's on it.

Sir Tim has a history and is always reported as being very wet, indecisive and wavering, vacillating with all his Government work. However, Sir Timothy is well known for being a good member of parliament particularly for his constituents. He understands how he can get voted back in at each election. Win a few local battles on local roads, nearby ekoles and some good victories on housing for the homeless. This politician 'gets it', his profile counts a lot at the local level. Good for him. He gets criticism at the national level, but in those jobs, who doesn't. I really like the sound of him from this email.

We can work together, this eminent MP and your Respectful Raconteur. What a chort.

I need to reply. I feel I am touching a nerve. Perhaps his daughter has been approached or even worse still, may be involved.

'Yes, Sir Timothy. I would be delighted to talk or even meet. I am available most days.'

A Digital Tomato gives me a deep and fulfilling interest. I enjoy it. It takes me into another world, a parallel existence. I was hoping Sally and I could develop it into the metaverse.

Back in reality, I feel I am perhaps there in the metaverse now talking with Sir Timothy, he is way out of my league and social standing, but who cares.

I cannot help thinking about Sir Timothy's motivation, perhaps not so worried about Sally but paranoid about his own daughter Alice. In which case, then Sally becomes a real case of importance for him, not a simple statistic.

With all this going on, I have difficulty concentrating on my programming. I make sure everyone is still looping and no-one is climbing to the top of Level 10 of Section 2 about to submit new demands on me to go to Section 3, as there is not a Section 3, yet. I need help.

Then there is Gio, the nerd, still looping in Level 8 of Section 1, poor little darling, issuing a writ on me.

My bank statements are showing I have about £8.5 million in all accounts. It has grown with the growing dimension of the jwet. What a chort. Yours candidly is a winner and will defeat Gio and the taxman, you gazzy. The success of my jwet and business, gives me such confidence. Lavi is not simple but with adequate resources behind you it makes you feel you are a winner and cannot be pushed around, nor beaten and defeated. Building up my own self-confidence I can talk on the same level with Sir Tim.

Hopefully, Sir Tim will turn up trumps, as well. Ping, surely not another message from him. Yes, here we go. 'Henrietta, can we talk later today or is this inconvenient? If not perhaps first thing tomorrow morning. Regards Sir Timothy.'

I am on a roll. My member of parliament wanting to talk to me on a Sunday evening. I cannot comprehend it. I koumense to believe his own daughter has been compromised. Why the urgency? Sir Timothy is on the case, that much is certain.

'Tonight at 6.00pm is excellent. Thank you. Henrietta.'

I listen to some more country and western. I rest not wishing to exert myself too hard in the meantime. I wait until 6.00pm when the fone goes.

'Is that Henrietta?' The stoodge has a posh voice. I need to keep up here.

'Yes, it is. Sir Timothy.' I try my best accent.

'Indeed.' A pause. 'Thank you so much for contacting me. I see your dilemma so clearly. I have an interest in this as a shadow immigration minister in the Home Office.'

'Yes Sir, I saw that in your profile.' Respect above all, Etta, give him respect.

'I have raised the issues in Parliament concerning the whole holistic matter on immigration. Especially settling these groups into a local area, wherever it may be. The foreign groups and we won't go any further there,' he has to be politically correct, for sure, 'that come over here and who expect a new life deserve better than we have given them since the 1950s. Think about it. I am concerned they bring their own local values and customs with them. They cannot move on into our society so quickly as we expect them to. They do not integrate properly into the UK along with our well tried and tested codes of behaviour and ethics, overnight. This is particularly relevant to the treatment of women. There are so many cases abroad and you only need to pick up the papers to see what goes on in, and I have to say, some of these misogynistic states. It is too easy to blame the immigrants.' Such salient words. He sounds so good.

Sir Tim has gone off beam here. I want to bring this back to the local police force, not the damn racist aspects and behaviour of so many. I do not think Sally's customer list, which certainly contained some foreign nons were doing any harm, just seeking their own personal gratification. It is the corrupt jakes we need to deal with in this instance. Sir Tom, get on to the right page, please.

'Exactly. Perhaps you should meet Sally, my friend. The girl accused of the murder and establish some basic facts of this particular case for yourself.'

'Good idea.'

'I know she is not your constituent, but I am. And I was being implicated.'

'Yes. She is in Surbiton police station, is that correct?'

'Yes, she is. And of course, the station is in your patch.' A wrong word, but sister you're getting on with Sir Tim so well, go for it and carry on.

'Exactly. I want to understand why the innocent young girl took it upon herself to murder this officer.'

'Sir Timothy. All will be revealed if and when you meet her. When will this be? Soon?' I try to pin him down.

'Tomorrow if I can move my diary around. And make space.'

Then I change path and involve his personal situation. 'How are your daughters doing, one is in Birmingham University, is that correct?'

'Yes, a little homesick, had a few issues, which of course worries her mother and me. You can imagine.'

'University is a time to grow up and become an adult, as scary as it may seem. I enjoyed it immensely and made some good friends and the course was fascinating, by the way.' I add this aspect otherwise his highness may think it was just a jolly.

'What did you study?'

'Computers, IT.' I do not want to let him know the full extent of my work and subsequent dark applications. I want him to concentrate on helping Sally.

'Tell me, how well do you know this, Sally?' Good, he is returning to the subject in hand. I do not wish to lead him on too much. It will sound too pushy. It seems on occasions I need to just guide him through.

'She is in the year below me and we became friends, we were on the same course. On various exercises. The university mix years from time to time. A form of practical testing, you know how it works.'

'And you have seen her in Surbiton police station?'

'Yes. I am afraid to report I found her in quite a mess. In my view she was beaten up, whether that was as a result of the fight she had with the victim or just passed off as such. But the wounds look very raw and recently incurred.'

'I see, anything else?'

'Well, Sir Timothy, I was dismayed at the treatment I personally received.' I take my opportunity. 'Sally had implicated me in the case as you know but the police gave me three, not one, but three therapists to speak to. They used funny and odd terms making out they were there to help me.'

'Did they?'

'I would not let them. I thought the whole thing extremely amateurish and a complete waste of time, not least the public dosh expended. Honestly, one was a general therapist.' I paused thinking I may be going too far with the whole sad, sorry and messy story. 'Then the next one was for anger management, she lasted all of five minutes and then ran out of the door and the last one was,' again I paused not for effect but to think. 'Mr Croft on some way out subject.' I could not bring myself to mention it. This may be something I can bring up later, perhaps when I speak with Sir Tim again. 'It seemed to me to be quite feeble.' In my own lespri I contrasted this experience to other treatments which had probably been given out in the past.

'I see,' he repeats. He is being very withdrawn but extracting information subtly from me all the while.

I take this pause to consider again why such an eminent local politician would be speaking with me on a Sunday evening. Little old me, your Respectful Raconteur, a twenty something girl from such a background living in suburbia, with dysfunctional brothers. A Pat and Mom of such a proletariat class with menial, humdrum, unskilled travats. Miss ordinary just trying to exist. A few bloods and no wish to mix or go out. Such a depressing lavi. Or perhaps this is where he gets his votes, helping the underclass. He is an experienced and canny politician, which works for me.

He continues, 'look, I shall be in touch. This is the best number to get you on? I will visit Sally tomorrow. As soon as I can in the morning. Goodbye for now.'

'Yes, it is. Bye. And oh, thank you very much for calling.'

'My pleasure.' He rings off.

There must be something behind this. He is taking a direct interest and he need not. There are probably many criminals who cross his path. Then there is Sally, not his constituent but in custody in his constituency. The chief must be one of his, and I could report him for unsatisfactory and unbecoming behaviour. I will let this lie until there is a better time. My word against his. Unless there are others he has preyed on. Sir Tim's daughter? Any of her friends? My imagination runs riot.

Then there is an email. It is Gio. 'Master, my father's law firm cannot find an address to serve this writ.'

My immediate reaction is to go back and say hard luck. An address, it is all winternet addresses now, we live in a digital world, Gio, don't you know? I choose to ignore this nerd once again. However, the email does remind me to search for a contract lawyer which I did promise to myself last night before I left the police station. The contract lawyer can confirm my position and legal status.

I wonder when Gio, the nerd, will let it go. Or is he proving something to Daddy? More dosh than sense. Come and live in my world for a few weeks. See if you like the constraints under which I lived the last twenty-four years, before creating A Digital Tomato. Living in this yard, the examinations I had to pass, the debt I incurred to educate myself. Such a struggle, but the fact I have had the initiative to create A Digital Tomato and made dosh is to my everlasting credit, such that I know how not to waste dosh. I think of Albie and now Gio. Wastemen.

Giovanni, you would not last a minute in my world. I choose not to reply and if they cannot find an address then there is no writ. Daddy's boy will have to tell his father. He will have to lose his £1, but this has to be more about pride. Yes, pride because he cannot leap Levels and go to Section 2. Let me see where he is. Oh, still on Level 8. Let me be vindictive and push him down to Level 6. Just be careful as you go.

No, I have a new idea, down to Level 5. Punish him, I enjoy this. Yes, turn right, well done Gio and whoosh, you slip slide right down to Level 5. This digital world can be compared to a modern-day Snakes and Ladders. You climb the ladders, you progress your career only to slip down the snakes. You make good and then the taxman, the five-o or a legal writ pushes you back down, slip sliding in a spiraling descent to be skrub, gubbled and in despair.

In lavi, you just must keep so strong. At times, I really do not think I have the will. I have placed all my bets on this allegedly wet MP, yet he sounded so helpful on the fone just now. I cannot help but to have my doubts. I hope I am wrong.

Then I receive an email from Sir Timothy Adam. 'Have you heard of Marshall Hall?'

I have not zord of this person, why should I? It, he or she must be famous.

I immediately research this character on the winternet.

<table>
<tr><td>

3

</td><td>

I am excited, I could not wait to find the entry on Marshall Hall. I am not sure why, but if the great and eminent Member of Parliament refers to it, then I must investi-gate. I do not have to wait long as it pops up

</td></tr>
</table>

almost immediately with so many references. I dissect the inter-esting bits.

Sir Edward Marshall Hall, KC (1858–1927) was an English barrister who had an anreta reputation as an orator. He success-fully defended many people accused of notorious murders and became known as 'The Great Defender'.

Marshall Hall practiced as a barrister in the late Victorian and Edwardian eras. This was when the public took a great interest in the sensational court cases of the day. This was over a century ago, but it all just seems so near. Big criminal and civil trials were widely reported on by the popular journals, on a daily basis. This is boom, and as a consequence, he and other suc-cessful barristers of the day became very famous. The widespread belief he was a much better orator than lawyer, may explain his failure to achieve elevation to the High Court, which was a source of great disappointment to this noble, educated stoodge. He clearly had his pushbacks as well, like me and Sally. But my sisters he must have lost some cases.

Born in Brighton, the son of an eminent physician Alfred Hall, Marshall Hall was educated at Rugby School and St Johns College Cambridge. Unusually, he left Cambridge after his fourth term to embark on what would now be regarded as a gap year, so very progressive at the time, in Paris and Australia, before returning to complete his law degree. In 1882 he married Ethel Moon. Is this what Sir Tim wants me to read? The marriage was unhappy. The couple were never compatible and were frequently separated. They were legally separated in 1889. The next year Ethel became pregnant by a lover and died of a botched abortion. A seamy very public lawsuit followed in which the lover, the abortionist and several others were indicted for Ethel's murder. Marshall Hall's guilt over his part in Ethel's fate would have a profound effect on his career; he would become famous for the impassioned nature of his defenses of chicks maltreated by bwoys. He subsequently married Henriette 'Hetty' Kroeger, with whom he had one daughter, Elan. This did not seem[1] very dramatic, but his attitude clearly changed. I wonder what I am heading towards, what happens next?

In November 1907 Marshall Hall was briefed on a case,

---

[1] All the references to Edward Marshall Hall and the details on the various cases are taken, with thanks, from Wikipedia. Reference https://en.wikipedia.org/wiki/Edward_Marshall_Hall. A donation has been made to Wikipedia in recognition of the source and its contribution to this story.

which contributed significantly towards his being painted with such titles as 'The Great Defender,' known as the Camden Town murder. On 12 September 1907, Bertram Shaw returned home during the evening to find his room locked. He borrowed a klef from a neighbour but upon entering was greeted with the horrific sight of his fiancee Emily Dimmock (known as Phyllis) lying naked on the bed, throat cut from ear to ear. She had been frigged. It was a savage but skillful attack on her from the nature of the wound. Nothing much had been taken from the flat, and the motive was a mystery; the case quickly became a sensation. Marshall Hall's spirited defense had persuaded almost all who were in court of the accused's innocence. This had caused a huge crowd to gather outside of court. Marshall Hall won and saved the accused from the gallows. This lawyer was a success story. If this is what Sir Tim is referring to, championing the under-class and defending women's rights, then I am totally on board.

However, he also successfully defended solicitor Harold Greenwood at Carmarthen Assizes in 1920. Greenwood had been accused of poisoning his wife with arsenic. Marshall Hall's cross-examination of the medical witnesses raised, at least, the possibility that Mrs Greenwood had died from an accidental overdose of morphine. His closing speech for the defense was described as 'the finest ever heard at the English bar.' The more impressive as Marshall Hall was seriously ill at the time.

I read on, completely engaged in the story of this lawyer. Equally successful was the defense Marshall Hall gave to Madame (or Princess) Marguerite Fahmy in 1923 for the shooting and subsequent death of her husband, Egyptian Prince Fahmy Bey at London's Savoy Hotel. He brought out the Prince's race and sexual habits, painting the victim as an evil foreigner who threatened 'white women' for sexual reasons. The jury accepted it. The Egyptian ambassador wrote several angry letters to newspapers criticizing Marshall Hall's blackening of the victim. There was more slur to come out of this for Marshall Hall, but the lawyer's success is what interests me. Is this why Sir Tim recommended the cases, the aspects on immigration? I am convinced by all these references, now.

However, this is getting more like it, a woman murdering a man.

But, and a big but just look what is reported next, my sisters. The case which caught my zyes is that of the Austrian-born prostitute Marie Hermann. She was charged with the murder of a client in 1894. Marshall Hall persuaded the jury that it was a case of manslaughter. Although he made full use of all his forensic skills, the case seems to be best remembered for his emotional plea to the jury – 'look at her gentlemen, God never gave her a chance, won't you?' I read this sentence many times and reflected.

Yes, that is exactly Sally's position. She never stood a chance.

I must read a few of his unsuccessful cases, it appears in 1901 he unsuccessfully defended Herbert Bennett in the Yarmouth Beach Case charged with strangling his wife. Marshall Hall was also given the brief to represent Dr Crippen at his trial in 1910. However, Crippen provided instructions that Marshall Hall did not feel comfortable with. As a result, Marshall Hall returned the brief and other counsel appeared at Crippen's trial. I think that would have been a loss leader and I am sure he wanted his case 'losses' compared to the 'wins' to be at a suitably low rate.

Let me concentrate on the matter in hand. Replace Marie with Sally, just 120 years later or thereabouts.

Hall was driven by the need to protect innocent women such as his first wife, Ethel. I can relate to this gentleman, so much. Sir Tim is directing me to the need to find a lawyer who can take this position for Sally. How can I? I should wait for Sir Tim to see Sally and establish the facts for himself. He should know a suitable lawyer.

Sir Tim said little on the specific case earlier in our call. He tried to keep it all at a high level and not commit himself. A politician to the end. I am unsure where all the cold press surrounding him comes from. I could search but decide not to do so. However, leading me on to this lawyer and the reported cases, he can clearly see the need for 'a Marshall Hall' in the 21st century. One who mixes with and emanates from a group of notorious criminal lawyers. Especially, these days, in the wake of various movements protecting women's rights. It is odd there is not a modern-day equivalent out there already. Perhaps there is, perhaps in America or another country abroad.

Of course, the complicating factor is the issue Sally murdered 'one of their own'. A fed and the profession, if you can call it such, gather closely together not to lose face. This needs careful management and where Sir Tim will need all his guile and experience to press for justice. He will press harder for justice than I ever can.

I send him a message.

'Sir Tim, (if I can be so bold), I must thank you for your interest. The Midlands police force are accusing the child trafficking sex ring to be a gang of immigrants in the area. A group who have come through the system. Your system. And perhaps, the police force are blaming the system for allowing this to happen. Like Prince Fahmy threatening white women, it is an easy hit.' I refer back to the great lawyer. 'Hence, we need to tread carefully. I look forward to talking to you after you have met with Sally.' I sign off.

There is no need to add any more. This puts it into a professional perspective for him and allows him to fight on behalf of the much-maligned immigrants. They may have different customs. They may not be as British as the rest of us, I relate to this, as a sovaj pesky quas skratty. They may have some faults but there is no reason to blame as cover for your own sexual gratification on to innocents. The five-o seem to me to have a lot to answer for. This disgusts me and I am so sorry for Inspector Bridgen, losing his life but if he was doing exactly as Sally says, he needs to be called out. Along with the stenky chief.

It is late Sunday and I can only wait for Monday morning now.

A little country and western does not go amiss. Pat and Mom have gone to bed. My eediat brothers are, guess what, down the pub, and yours candidly has made progress.

I want to tell Sally, my bestie, I just might be able to help her. I cannot contact her as her fone has been taken away from her. I am sure the visit from Sir Tim in the morning will give her hope and she will know from that very action, I have been doing what I can from this side of the huge imaginary line which now divides us.

I mentioned the therapists to Sir Tim, but not the awful predatory approach from the chief, the inspector, the rapacious and grasping Pendlebury with the awful stenk of aftershave. It brings back such totoy memories.

I need time to think. Johnny Cash walks the line, Jim Reeves welcomes me to his world and Roy Orbison drives all night. Gran Betty enjoyed Johann Sebastian so much. She was an expert on the world of classical music. I need to hold on to whatever strength I can. I need to find an incredible example to all youths of today. Perhaps Gran Betty was the example.

My thoughts wander to the other young girls in the Midlands area. When you deal with authority you clearly think them to be fine, good, upstanding and beyond reproach. These officers are not. I wonder if Sir Tim knows this. He can go in on the pretense of defending the immigrants, which is good. I am lying here thinking his very own daughter must have suffered.

An email from Gio. He is reminding me to supply an address for the writ. I should reply asking if he has got back to Level 8 yet. Let me look and there he is wandering around Level 5. I can push him down a Level. Go straight on there, Gio, oops be careful. You slipped down a Level with that choice. Such a shame. I am not a nasty person but someone like Gio puts me in that mood and he caught me at the wrong time, too.

'I notice you are now at Level 4 of Section 1. Is there something wrong with your method or approach? I am contacting my lawyers shortly. As I have said a few days ago, I can repay you the £1 entrance fee.' That should keep him guessing.

I do not expect to zor from Mrs Dharsanny, for a day or two.

Pat and Mom are about to start another busy week as wage slaves. They are asleep or at least in bed.

Then the front door goes. My brothers return early. Either drunk, been bataying or out of dosh. Or all twa.

A knock at my bedroom door.

From outside comes the voice. 'Sis, are you awake? It's Cyril.'

'Come in.' I am fully dressed.

'Thanks.' And with that the thin, ugly Cyril stands in front of me. 'Sis, I want to get on in life. I am fed up being where I am, just a loser going down the pub every night.'

'Right.' I do not know what to say. 'Where's Albie?' I muse quickly to myself Cyril is after the monthly insurance premium dosh for his new car so he can at least learn to drive it.

'I left him there.'

'I have never known you de to be separated.'

'I know. I told him straight. Our lives are currently a journey to nowhere. You must be doing something on your kompyuter and making some dosh.'

'OK. Let's talk in the morning, I have had a busy day and need dodo. I think I am still recovering from the day spent in the police station.' Saying the right things to Sir Tim had drained me. Trying to be tactful to Cyril yet making my point on all the facts and eliciting his help will be exhausting and is not for now.

'That is fine, sis.'

Cyril shuts my door and I feel very much at ease with the

world. For my eediat brother to want to understand what he can do, is a breakthrough. Believe me. Whether anything comes of it or not, it does not matter. It is currently a huge step forward. I look forward to Monday. I fall into a deep kabicha.

'Look at her gentlemen, God never gave her a chance, won't you?' Marshall Hall's emotional plea to the jury haunts me. Zonbis are in and around my tet.

4

I wake wondering how the meeting will go between Sally and Sir Tim, if it will actually take place today and, if it does, how long it will last. I sincerely trust he can access the dunfa today, if not very soon. She has spent another day at the hands of the five-o. My heart goes out to her. I know she killed Bridgen, but circumstances prevailed at the time for her to do so. I gave her a lot of konsey when I was at university not to follow such a course of action to get dosh. She was hellbent to do it and I think overall she got off on it. She enjoyed the excitement and thrill of the meetings. I was her defans to ensure she was protected. It was always taught to us in sex education at ekole that the loving was more important than the sexual act, itself. I think she forgot this and just had the dosh to survive daily life at university, in her own panses.

I must admit it was my idea to take the small, sharp, pointed and very effective screwdriver. She used it and used it well. As a result, she is going through hell now, but I am so really proud of her. I want her working with me in my business, for that much, I am now so very sure.

Then I think about Cyril, no rush to act there, but he seems to be in remorse. It may be for the nicking of my credit card dosh. Strange boy and perhaps deeply affected by his twin, the abnormal, eccentric, curious and bizarre Albie. My problem, here, thinking this through is, if I engage Cyril, Albie comes along as an adjunct. I do not get one brother, I get two. I need to continue to push this out and take my time with Cyril, engage but not hire. Just let him know I am interested in helping. A resolution comes to me quite quickly, I can give him menial tasks and pay him a salary above his benefit cheques, this way he will think he is involved. He was a good lad when he came to the police station with my kompyuter. I will give him that much credit. Albeit I think he was being nosey and all that. By contrast, Albie was nowhere to be gazzied.

I can talk to Cyril later today, if not later in the week.

My priority is Sally. In my view, she is no chung. The outcome of her case and her future trial will stay with me for some years to come. I know this for sure. I must do everything I can to help, and help is required right now.

Then there is a wapp. It is from Sir Tim. The stoodge I am waiting to zor from. 'Henrietta, I have been in the police station earlier today to see Sally. She is OK. A few bruises which seem to me to be very recently afflicted. The way she is being treated does not make me happy at all. In fact, quite disgusted.' Wow, he sounds as if he is getting ever more deeply into this case. Also, most importantly on side with me. 'She spoke at length. I have news for you, can we meet?'

I do not need a second invitation. 'Of course, where and when?'

'My surgery office and perhaps at 11.00am, I have other matters to attend to before then and to make a few calls.' I struggle to understand why members of parliament call their biwos located in their constituencies surgeries. It is as if they are like doctors and those who attend are suddenly going to get better, fixed miraculously or all their ills mended just and only by attending. I must record with you the word surgery grates with me. Just call it a biwo. 11.00am works, I have nothing else on.

'I shall be there.' Sir Tim then replies, kindly providing me with the address, which I already knew, of course.

Why is this MP considered wet and ineffectual as he has been nothing other than immediate with his help and full of action. The public persona is so different to what you find up close and personal. I read up on his history and voting record. When Labour were in power he rebelled more times than he voted for the government, that is a good reason to be maligned, I suppose. I like the independent thought and action, though. He may be considered wet by his colleagues but to me he is a saviour. A right proper person from authority.

I notice from the winternet Sir Timothy Adam was involved in a scrape with the Metropolitan police. It was five years ago and he was caught bewing and chofering. There seemed to be considerable fog and obscurity about the case. He had been bewing late in the members bar at the Houses of Parliament. Never a good sign, possibly buying favours with all that entails. He left the bar with a younger colleague. Someone tipped the police off when he was leaving. He went to his car in the underground car park and sat in the driver's seat. He had not started the engine but his klefs were in the ignition as if he was about to do so. It was then the Metropolitan Police stepped in. They say for his own good. He said he was calling a chauffeur to come and take him home. On the one hand he was caught red handed in charge of a vehicle on the other hand he had not driven it. Make of this what you will but it seems to me it is avaricious policing and overkill. He was charged and fined. He had twelve months not driving, given a warning about his behaviour and suffered public shame, a hard lesson learnt. It did pass over quickly.

I recollect the call last evening and his intent interest. He is very non-committal but I just think to myself he has to have lots at stake in this case. Fundamentally, there has to be a personal interest here. Is it the maligned immigrants and his career, his family with something surrounding Alice or just a vendetta against the police due to his previous recent run-in. Or all three?

He is coy about the significance this very case presents him, but he is taking a direct and very personal interest. Which is good for Sally and me.

I start to get ready. I wonder what he will think of my orange cheve. At least my finger and toe-nails match, today. I chort at myself. Getting all dolled up to meet the eminent Sir Timothy Adam. I have to question my change in attitude, but I still make up.

The pictures on my walls mean so much to me. They are my motivating force. The work of Salvador Dali, the free imaginative spirit is just wonderful.

Then, I remember I want to see a lawyer. I have time before

I leave to meet for Sir Tim. Researching on the winternet I find there is one close to Sir Tim's offices. I send an email explaining my dilemma with the angry nerd Gio. The fact I have chargin terms and conditions for my jwet and the fact I wish to repay the £1 entrance dosh. They come back almost immediately with a full set of terms and conditions. Has no-one anything else to do? I sign these and send the lawyer £2,000 on account of fees. I notice and always recall at university the law students saying lawyers and accountants are only interested in fees. Probably because they have nothing to sell other than their precious time. This should keep them happy. No reply, so I decide to call in on my way back after my meeting.

I touch the silver-frame as I leave my room. I am ready for this. Cyril is in the hallway.

'Sis, any thoughts?'

'Yes, lots, just bear with me while I have to sort out the Sally issue first.'

'Sure, sis. Can I help though? Where are you going this time, I just want to make sure you are safe? You know, Pat and Mom were scared out of their wits on Saturday.'

'I understand. I am a big girl and know what I am doing, OK.' I say with a somewhat sarka tone to my larenks.

'Not really fair to put them all through this, is my view, and Albie wants to come along with me, too.' Those words sting me like a bee. I know it was not going to be one of them, but both. They come as a package. I could not wait to leave the house. It is if they were driving me away. In all innocence they were so successful at that, without even knowing. I walk past the fowzy Cyril and slam the front door. I hope he receives the message fo and clear.

I catch the 256 bus. It goes right along the high street and there is a stop near Sir Tim's biwo, or surgery, and the lawyers are close, too, good. I can pop in after, if only to meet the person assigned to the case. With £2,000 in their anpoche they could send an answer to plum nerd Gio. I can then keep my anonymity. Wait to see what Gio's crowd say. So much going on.

Everyone is looking at my tet and orange cheve. It suits my complexion. I alight the bus. Walk a few yards and there is the surgery.

A fairly non-descript shop. With all red stickers plastered all over it, saying 'Labour' their red rose and the latest slogan. 'In it together.' We are certainly in it, but time will tell if it is together. I wonder what this was before, a butcher's or a shoe repairer's, whichever it has two matching window sides to it. I expect my famous MP is in there. I am unsure why he is there today, I thought Mondays to Thursdays were for parliament and Fridays were set aside for constituents, but anyway he has accommodated me immediately and for this fact alone, I am extremely pleased.

I enter and there in front of me is an elderly, thin, smart, secretarial-looking lady.

'I have come to meet Sir Tim at 11.00am today.'

'Oh, yes, we were expecting you, please take a seat. He will be with you shortly.' She beckons to the three unoccupied yet so very uncomfortable looking seats opposite her. I look at the clock and see I am early, it is just 10.50am, which is good. Not too early to show I am too keen, but timely enough to show I am disciplined and so very much on the case.

Then the door opens and out walks the gentleman I seek. He is medium height, a little overweight and with a somewhat greasy mug and cheve. He is grey, showing the age or the responsibility and lifestyle is taking its toll. His suit is blue, his tie a bright company red, and his shirt is white.

'Henrietta,' he greets me. 'Please come in. I like your orange hairstyle, quite remarkable.' We walk into his office together.

'Thank you to both.' I sit down in front of his desk. So many books behind him he surely could not have read them all. It must be for show to impress. I just hope he is going to be good to his word. But then he has not promised anything, I am already anticipating too much resulting from this meeting. I look around his office and as expected pictures of Tony Blair, Harold Wilson and Clement Atlee. The leading, recent and famous Labour Prime Ministers. Ramsay Macdonald, James Callaghan and Gordon Brown are missing. I know my history. Wilson was in charge in the 1960s when the youth rampaged the country always bataying and things. Socialism does not create change. It has left the young behind just like the Tories. This is not party political but cultural. Hope and aspiration are two words no political party recognizes. The rhetoric is the same from them all and all the time, sisters. Beware.

'Very nice to meet you. Thank you for bringing this nasty matter to my attention.'

'That is fine, but I have to say I have found your prompt response a little, well,' I stutter, 'a little overwhelming.'

'I am not surprised, but I do care about my constituents. They are all to a man and woman important to me. After all, they vote me into this job every four or five years.' He looks down at me somewhat condescendingly while saying this, but I can take it, if it gets me to my end game. 'I respect them and try to help where I can.'

'Thank you.'

'Let me tell you why I am so interested. You were taken into custody because of your contact and friendship with Sally.' I nod to him. 'Totally understandable, but I need to tell you something. Chief Inspector Pendlebury is not from here.' I wonder about the relevance and importance. 'He is in charge of and head of the Midlands police force. Bridgen was operating under his orders.'

'He is one of them.' I am stunned. I could have kicked myself for not hacking the winternet. I am losing my focus, so consumed by everything else and helping Sally I had missed the obvious.

'Exactly, one of them.' The MP's words are creating too many riddles for me. I need to unravel the word 'them' and ask some straight questions.

'What does this mean?'

'It means, Henrietta, whatever Bridgen was up to or doing, Pendlebury knew and condoned.'

'If Bridgen was involved in child trafficking then Pendlebury knew.' I seek assertions.

'Yes.' Sir Tim pauses. 'My daughter Alice came home a week ago, in tears. A terrible, upsetting and senseless mugging of a young girl resulting in the loss of her purse which left her compromised at the police station begging to be let out.' He pauses. 'Luckily, she mentioned me, her father. They checked their records, believed her, backed off and let her go. Her mother and I were distraught.'

'That itself is wonderful news. You could help her.' I presume Alice was confronted because she was young, in need and in despair. Exactly the type of prey the so-called vultures scavenged for in the Midlands area. 'We need to do something huge here.' I stop talking.

Sir Timothy Adam looks at me. 'Hence, I am not surprised there are other cases.' We both understand the meaning of his words. Then he adds. 'Lots, perhaps.' He comes across to me as forlorn, lost and a little worried by the complexity and vastness of the prospect in front of him.

I sit there in full shock such that I cannot bouche. There is so much more to this than I even contemplated a day ago, three days ago or even when I zord the terrible news from Coventry.

This is a mess. Is it too much for Sir Timothy to handle, I panse to myself.

I wait for him to gather his emotions and thoughts and to continue talking.

	I sit in his biwo in silence, waiting for him
	to speak. The news hits me hard. It is little
5	wonder Sir Tim is onside with this case and
	Sally's search for help. Shortly, it will be
	time for me to let him know about the chief

and his sal unsolicited approach to me.

Sir Tim looks at his fone and then at me and adds. 'Your friend Sally has now been moved to a hospital for treatment. She is safe.' He smiles.

The actions and remedies being put in place by this MP in less than 24 hours are really amazing. I cannot be more grateful. Sally must be so thrilled and feeling at last her plight is easing. There even may be an end, a good resolution in sight for her.

'Can I go and visit her?'

'No, best not to. She is under police guard there, with the hospital staff running around and tending to her. At least, I do think there will be no further beatings. Not any further mal-treatment. I would be surprised if it took place now.'

'This happened, right? You are sure she is in hospital and safe.' Naturally, I seek full reassurance.

'For sure.'

There is a pause.

'You haven't fully explained how you are so deeply passionate about this matter or why you are really helping me?' I ask thinking to myself either he harbours a deep hatred of the police and their methods, he wishes to protect his immigration policy, or his daughter did suffer. While help is at hand and help from a powerful source and ally, I need confirmation his motive is genuine. I take the opportunity rightly or wrongly to press him on this issue.

'I shall leave it at that for the moment, Henrietta.' The stoodge closes the conversation down and shuts up like a clam. 'I hope I have helped and suggest we keep in touch with any developments or progress. Alice is OK, too.' An unexpected reference to his daughter.

'OK. Thank you. I shall be on my fone.' With these words I shake the MP's hand realizing it is my prompt to leave his biwo, nodding farewell to the officious looking secretary on my way out. Who acts as the MP's own defans, sitting in the front office, just like the fed I had in front of my yard on Friday night.

I am extremely disappointed I could not press for more information, but so far so good. Sally is safe, or rather safer for the moment. I have already achieved a considerable amount.

Outside on the pavement, I light up a brown. I feel real boom, possibly the best I have for some months. The authorities in the form of this eminent MP, a shadow minister, are onside. Fortuitously or not, he saw the predicament and could add his weight to the matter. Many have doubts about Sir Tim, but everything he has achieved in this case has been exemplary. I take a long drag of the brown. Possibly the authorities can be beaten. I am starting to take enormous pleasure from these thoughts. I spark the air. I no longer feel alone. The brown makes me feel at ease with the whole wide world. Odd, he did not once mention Marshall Hall, perhaps this will be later. I am sure he knows a reputable solicitor for Sally. I left some things out there, too.

The jakes, the therapists, the events at the police station and everything I had suffered in all innocence only two days earlier can be defeated. Those responsible will be crushed and hopefully all the sour events long forgotten.

I jump on a return bus 256 to head home. My orange cheve, turning heads and making people talk under their breath make me chort. I get off and walk up my garden path, next door's chat goes running away. I shoo it back to where it belongs. I put the klef in the door and then have an awful thought. I did not go into the solicitor's office. I forgot with all the excitement of knowing I had helped Sally. My emotions had run wild and taken over. What a morning's work, so involved and subsumed with the objectives. The lawyer and my reply to little Gio will have to wait.

All I want now is to get Pendlebury by the bubbles and I believe I am on the track. Sally is still my important issue. I will not let her down. I must not lose sight of this.

Having rushed to my haven, I look at Salvador Dali's melting clocks, the silver-frame. I think of Gran Betty, Pat and Mom and those eediat brothers. They have all made me what I am. I am sensitive, perhaps too sensitive, but I only want justice. Tinedje life is not good. Sisters, I repeat little hope nor aspiration exists for tinedjes. These are all the aspects which made those in the past batay with their frers in banns. There are many banns if you look for them. Dealing in draws or weed and trying to make their living and dosh through harming tinedje life. I hate it.

Sisters, I hate it all.

I search and hack the winternet. My word, Sir Tim is right, Pendlebury is in the Midlands force. I am annoyed once more I did not seek this information earlier and hack their files sooner. I am losing my sharp edge. Wait a minute, Alice Adam was interviewed as her purse and belongings were stolen. The crime files back everything up. Sir Timothy Adam is telling the truth, he is to be completely trusted now. I am so pleased. A thrill comes over me. Trust is a small yet important word.

I trust Sir Timothy.

I panse to myself, Sir Tim, you do have your work cut out. You are my larenks in parliament and in the wide world. We can win and beat the lot of them.

I think about my own environment. The house is quiet. My brothers in their own room. Pat possibly working a shift and Mom almost certainly packing her goods. I must ask her one day what she packs. I keep forgetting that as well. It always escapes my lespri when I talk to her, probably as we are always on another important subject. I expect the goods are important. She makes it seem as such. I look at my messages after I settle down with a cup of cha.

There is a holding reply from my lawyer, I cannot help thinking ill of him, the leech. At least he is not asking for more fees. There is nothing further from Gio the nerd. My brothers have gone quiet. No messages from them, the plum tinedjes. Mrs Dharsanny has not replied but then I do not expect one from her. It must have been a record turn around last week for the government tax office to reply within one day. I am sure she needs authority from above to adhere to my request. Why is there always someone in authority, or supposedly higher than you to make a decision? This society sucks.

I look at A Digital Tomato and it all seems so stupid now. I am falling out of love with my jwet, my baby. I have made my dosh and to develop another Level is a stretch or a mile too far. I can leave everyone looping in Section 2, why should I bother, when you get unappreciative nerds like Gio. It hurts. I will leave it alone, especially if Sally does not come into the business. The metaverse seems a distant prospect, now – I was late to a party that hadn't even started yet!

There are too many unanswered questions right now. I know I am feeling extremely unsettled. I want Sally to be better, for her to face no trial for killing Bridgen, and for Sir Tim to settle the score with Pendlebury.

Until these things happen, I do not think I can concentrate on anything else.

I turn to my country and western. A little Jim Reeves. There is someone who was making merry music in the long and distant past. 'Welcome To My World,' favourite from the silver and slippery larenks of Gentleman Jim. I lie on my bed. I want time to pass quickly, I am impatient. I need resolution.

The critical issue to me is this, since my release Saturday

night, there is no word, nothing from the boys in blue. Nothing. Silence. Even if they did want to see me again, I have my protection ring, now. Not Pat nor Mom, not my brothers, but Sir Tim. I will vote for him forever. I do not care about his beliefs nor any madcap policy nor party he may follow or be involved with, but his care and attention to my own predicament and case is beyond anything I could expect. I am extremely and very pleasantly surprised. I sleep a while.

I wake up with a bang of the front door, it must be Mom back from travat and her packing. I have dozed for two hours and Gentleman Jim has long finished.

It crosses my lespri I would have achieved nothing if Sir Tim had not come to my aid. Does the legal system and the aid on offer extend to this type of case? I research legal aid which was not brought in until 1950 or thereabouts. Very much in its infancy in the 1960s when help was only considered to be given out by stoodges walking around in whitecoats. The experts. Delving further into the winternet the Legal Aid, Sentencing and Punishing Offenders Act cut funding from nearly one million cases a year in half. Therefore, to obtain such funding to defend oneself is even yet more difficult to achieve these days. It seems it is a lowly paid exercise for the solicitors who embark on this field. Fancy always mixing with badmen and then getting nothing for it. Being awakened, if not on call, at 2.00am on a Sunday morning as a drunk is disorderly and causes havoc. Only then to attend the police station and find it is one of your regulars who you habitually get off their crime, but who never learns.

It must be awful for those highly qualified lawyers. I am fed up with people. I contrast this to Sir Tim who is such a bright and shining light in the darkness of human mediocrity.

It is all very odd indeed, reducing legal aid is hardly the action of a considerate and caring government. The more I investigate the more everything can be brought into question. The little man, the ordinary citizen is always punished. We are all dunfas in society. Caught, sentenced and trapped.

The law is an ass. A terrific satire. It all completely stenks.

Frustrating the legal process is easy and perhaps this is a route I can take if Sir Tim does not win through. There must be alternatives open to me. I do not know what they may be right now. However difficult, I must try them for Sally and not least for my own pride. I struggle to think of anything while I embark on this route with Sir Tim. He needs to find and recommend to me today's actual Marshall Hall. That's it.

At this point in time, I shall back all my hopes on Sir Tim. I have to. As I did that day at Newbury. I chort to myself.

I receive an email from the lawyer. 'Henrietta, we have reviewed the case and feel the protest group do have a case against you. In your terms and conditions, you mention the prize money which prima facie means they have a case to be able to win while playing the game. Can you provide me with a list of the winners, their names and addresses. This is extremely important to show there are some winners in A Digital Tomato.' I break off and panse. Yours candidly is a winner. 'Please reply as soon as you can and then I can draft a reply to Giovanni. He seems hellbent on making this an example case.' I agree with that much Mr Lawyer I cannot shake him off, always on my zepol. 'If we can prove he is incompetent at the jwet and a sore loser, then I feel we have a case,' the legal man concludes. Perhaps these lawyers are on my side as well. They should be, after all I did pay them handsomely.

Well, that is good, within one letter or ten lines the advice changes from no hope to possible. I read it again and conclude why do I bother with these people?

I look at my records and compile the list and send it to him, with another £2,000 on account of fees to keep them happy and onside. Further payment should help.

I open my door. I zor Pat and Mom bouching in the kitchen. I do not wish to partake as they will certainly ask again about my impending move.

I lie on my bed. I fall into a deep dodo. Sisters, everything is falling into place.

<table>
<tr><td>6</td></tr>
</table>

It is now Tuesday morning. I look out into the back garden. It is a bright and sunny day. The world, my own world, could not be better. I am home, both warm and safe. I will pop down to the kitchen soon for some breakfast.

My lawyer is dealing with Gio. Mrs Dharsanny is all quiet and my bestie, Sally, is in good hands being helped. I get up, I turn on my kompyuter and there are no messages. The outside world is all quiet, at peace with itself as well. No one wants to bother yours candidly, your Respectful Raconteur. At this moment in time, anyway.

I look at my room and all around me, in all its glory. The silver-frame needs dusting and I attend to this, it shines and sparkles after a vit rub. I feel proud. I feel as if I have lived up to my parans' standards. They obey authority as we all should, albeit it is not always easy. I admire their resolve. As I have said before in this dosye, I am not punk, as sisters, you can now tell. Pat and Mom seem to have gotten over my incident with the feds. At least the treatments I received were soft and gentle and quite honestly pathetic. I know those in times gone by were more aggressive. How the world turns? Not always for the better. As I grow older, I think and am inclined to consider more that way.

I drink my hot lait and it goes down smoothly. I look at all the emails and messages over the last few days, just to consider them again and update myself where I am. Then one pops into my inbox from the lawyer. Overnight he has constructed a great reply to Gio and the protest group. Basically, it is a 'go away' letter, but one which I feel is polite and meaningful. It states my position and can only be taken as such by the stoodges supporting this nerd. Go away. Here is the list of the winners, you are not one of them and by the way, good luck in the future. I am refunding your losses of £1 and suck on that. I chort to myself at the legal language and the caveats and excuses. Hardly layman's language. It is hilarious and it confirms to me the lawyers make an okabine of everything. This letter is first rate evidence of the fact.

I approve the letter and hope it achieves a resolution. I say so in my reply to the lawyer, with abundant thanks, of course.

Some country and western is required. I do not want to look at A Digital Tomato, as I said yesterday to you all, until my bestie is involved with me, I think I have fallen out of love with the jwet despite it being a chargin goldmine. My bank accounts have risen slightly to £8.7 million, which is good. It is a shame my attitude to my virtual baby has changed so much. Everything has a shelf life including us humans. Perhaps I would feel the same if I did donnen a chick. I may get fed up with him or her. Too much mess in my lespri. Too much responsibility and effort. Perhaps Miss

Chambers, Miss Archer and Mr Croft were right. I may need help. To help yourself you need to at first realise it yourself.

Then I see an email arrive in my inbox from Sir Tim. This is important. I open it. 'Henrietta, Sally is recovering well. I am speaking to the Home Office minister today in respect of her case. I really hope we can reduce the charge to manslaughter and with extenuating circumstances. It appears the Home Office are reviewing the cases of the police officers in the Midlands. This is all very interesting stuff. I must admit I have to leave it there. For protocol and privileged information purposes, I cannot say too much more to you. Please bear with me and, of course, trust me on this.' He signs off wishing me well.

I am thrilled with the update from him. It appears everything, such as matters decided in higher echelons of power and in the bigger circles of authority, to which yours candidly is not privileged, are starting to kick into action. It is all good news. I do trust him. He has proven this time and time again. I do not need to do any hacking at this juncture. No second guessing. Wheels are turning and the right people are being advised. This is chargin. I start to think about all the younger generations who were around when we did not have the winternet and such immediate information. Was it better or worse? Then to everyone since then, who have been so badly let down by the state. Perhaps Sir Tim and his cronies can champion their causes in the future. More of this for later.

I know Sir Tim is interested in his immigration policy and those policies of the Government. He is at least speaking up for the appropriate and correct settlement procedures. I saw this on the winternet. That is a noble approach, I like it. It shows he cares. One day perhaps he may be the minister and not the shadow. And I know him. I know him very well, and how proud am I?

I decide to answer Sir Tim. 'Thank you and I look forward to hearing any updates and news. Henrietta.'

My need for a brown is overwhelming. I look for my packet and see it is in my coat anpoche. I touch the picture of the melting clocks for a reality check. I drag on the brown hanging out of the window. Next door's chat runs across our lawn and under the fence into its own garden. I wonder if chats think. They must. This one is running from another one. It is bigger and looks stronger and a thug. I do not recognize this particular new chat on the block, but it is definitely aggressively chasing next door's chat. In their world it is a simple matter of chasing the weakest or humblest. No animal rights and protection amongst the chats. I see the big chasing chat struggles to get under the fence and in fact it struggles to get through but does so eventually. This gives next door's time to escape into their yard. The big chat gives up, like most of us in life. I start to shoo it away. It then cleans itself down after extracting itself from the fence and somewhat humiliated, strolls back across the garden to whence it came. It is agile enough to jump back onto the wooden compost box which houses all the grass cuttings from our lawn, hops onto the top of the shed and over and out into the big wide world. The distraction for this morning ceases. I have also finished my brown.

Returning to my screen I see an email from the one and only, the great Mrs Dharsanny. So far so good this morning, Gio,

Sally and I including next door's chat all sorted. The taxman is next in line, yours candidly is winning all the way through, today.

'Dear Sir or Madam, thank you for your recent letter.' Always remain polite. 'We have considered your offer and have to say it is an interesting one.' Again, a great opening, where is this going? 'In order to alleviate yourself from any further scrutiny and to join our whistleblowing team, we would like to accommodate your offer. In order to do this, we would ask that you pay £75,000 to us on account of the taxable earnings from the alleged winnings at Newbury. Let me explain our rationale. This is because we consider it to be a trade and a profession. It is therefore taxable as income to you. We have taken the current rates of tax and a personal allowance into account and arrived at this settlement figure. The calculation is attached.' I look at it and it seems in order. I calculate this to be in the region of 30% of my declared earnings. That is harsh but fair. I read on. 'If you agree with this then we can issue the forms for you to become a whistleblower. On receipt we then arrange for an Inspector to meet with you to discover those earning in the darknet through what we may label illegal or illicit trades and making profits thereon. Two officers will accompany the Inspector.' Then the usual sign offs.

What an interesting letter, I panse. I have them on the run. Considering yours candidly could be looking at a tax bill in the region of over £3 million then this is a quality deal. They seek tax, no doubt, to balance things in their books. I konprann this much. Then I stitch all those in Emarq. I like it. It sits well with me. It proves to me I have a conscience.

Tuesday is becoming mega Tuesday. I am certainly winning all the way through. I email Mrs Dharsanny. I do not wish to look too keen. 'I was expecting this kind of offer and thank you very much. Hence, I can respond extremely quickly. Please send me the forms. I look forward to completing them and meeting with your officers. I realise I will need to settle the £75,000 promptly please provide me with the payment co-ordinates.' With the usual sign offs I press the button and it is sent. Wonderful, such another huge problem off my back.

I lie on my bed and listen to some music. Time passes by. Perhaps I doze a little more.

This allows me to really think and concentrate about Sally and her well-being. I hope she is recovering well, but physically it has only been two days so perhaps it may be more her mental state and health which is recovering. I look on the winternet where the hospital is. I could get a taxi there and barge in to see her. I wonder what she will say. Sally must be pleased with the progress I have made so far. I am confident she knows it is my doing. It is such a shame we cannot be in contact. I think I shall wait a day or two, it has been a lot for her in these last few days and I do believe, reading between the lines of Sir Tim's comments from first thing this morning, she may need some recovery time from the aggie she has received from the five-o of all people. But what do you expect, Bridgen was one of their own.

Suddenly my phone pings and a news alert comes through. I read it.

'MP found on Clapham Common in an indecent act with a minor.' What the hell? I had put a news alert on Sir Tim.

Anything he did or was reported in the news or papers, social media or wherever, would come through to me. No prompt in place for any other MP. It has to be him. 'Long-standing Labour Shadow Minister for Immigration and the Surbiton constituency Sir Timothy Adam has been found by police procuring underage prostitutes for his own self-gratification. This is after months of an undercover police operation, known as Operation Clapham. A gang soliciting these young people operates in South London and the police have made many dawn raids today and are holding eight people in custody.'

My world is at an end. I am totally deflated.

It continues. 'Sir Timothy and any of his family have refused to comment on the story. The Inspector leading the operation reported a man was found in a compromising position mid-morning today in the public toilets on Clapham Common with a well-known and previously convicted prostitute from Romania aged 17. Police had been tracking them for weeks.' My hacking skills could not have broken this firewall even if I had tried. 'It is understood the man had connections with Government immigration records and could make contact with the other, underage party. Police report this activity has been ongoing for some while. While the police would not name Sir Timothy Adam MP we understand his office in Surbiton is closed and all access to him via social media or email is prohibited. An official statement from the Labour party will follow shortly.'

I reflect on what I have read and read it again and again and then again. I sit down.

That is it, I vitly analyse, my game is up.

There is no hope for Sally. What a nasty, creepy, two-faced dillbat this Tim Adam is. The future will mean he will no longer be a knight of the realm, no longer an MP and most importantly to me no longer of any help nor influence with Sally and her case. I am totoy with rage and have desperate thoughts. Devastated I just stare at the wall in front of me. I am motionless for some while.

Sisters, I actually do not know what to do next.

When I gather myself, my immediate thought is, was this MP in it all along with the police? Surely not. Was he trying to blackmail the police and get onside by intervening with Sally? Then, I think about the story about Alice, this may mean otherwise or perhaps the Midlands police made a genuine mistake. My brenn is wandering but overall, the fact he could have access to susceptible people through the immigration records means he did not have to be working alongside the police. He had other means of access to the victims. This is terrible news and absolutely disgusting. He probably only wanted to get involved with me and help Sally to see if he needed to cover up any links. Perhaps his daughter, once compromised, started to realise her father was implicated. He may have been instigating the links of the police with the sex gang.

I shall never know. It is all too dark and murky and why bother to go there. Sir Tim is history now.

Do I care about any business which does not affect me? No, but my panses are with Sally, poor kid.

I sit stunned, quiet and appalled for some time. Who do

you trust? Who can I trust? Probably no one. They are all in it. Power, they all say, corrupts and of that I am now absolutely convinced.

I just hope he gets what he deserves, such a fall from grace too but this is immaterial to not only what he has done but also who he has let down. His family, his associates, his constituents. Alice may not have the wedge now to go to university and she may end up like Sally. Who knows?

Then, and only then, my panses go back to Sally and her plight. Once out of hospital she will be charged, put on trial and sentenced for certain. She has no hope, perhaps I should go down to the hospital and barge in and try my luck that way.

I must.

I rise from the bed, get ready and charge downstairs. I have ordered a cab, and I explain to the stoodge chofing it that I need to go to the hospital. He chofers at some speed through Surbiton and we arrive quicker than I could imagine.

I pay the driver and rush into the hospital. They have no record of Sally, they must have, I do not believe them. I sho-chan at the receptionist and she turns away. She says dis and dat to me. Another arrives, I shochan at her as well. It turns out Sally was discharged back to the police station only thirty minutes earlier. Life always hinges on such small defined flashes in time. The wrong time and the wrong place and all hope for a good turn-out ends there and then.

Sally will be charged for murder. Marshall Hall's words stick with me, 'look at her gentlemen, God never gave her a chance, won't you?' It is the same for the young, Romanian chung.

This world is so sad. Why did they find themselves in that position? Others put them there. People traffickers and the person in authority took advantage.

I get marched off the hospital premises by security.

To defuse the situation, I decide to call a taxi and go home.

It all depresses me so much. What started to be such a great day quickly turns out otherwise.

<table>
<tr><td>

7

</td><td>

Since the abortive hospital visit six months has passed. I moved out of Pat and Mom's house almost immediately afterwards. I bought a little flat in the town centre of Guildford. I just had to get away from

</td></tr>
</table>

Surbiton. Not so much from my family but all the memories of those few days. The flat has three bedrooms, in line with my original plan to be with Sally. We can use this flat and work together here, that is, if she is ever let out and wishes to take on any proposal with me developing my business. The future and the metaverse have such wonderful possibilities in the game industry. We would have been such early adopters. That I know, but I need help. Sisters, who else is there?

The flat is comfortable I need not describe it, as you can imagine it. It is on the first floor which enables me to feel secure. My study or office is not my bedroom and I look out onto the communal gardens, so effectively it feels very much like the yard in Surbiton, but more space. I have all my country and western streams and lists with me. The important stuff to me remains just the same as it ever was, if not more so.

It is all very drab around here, though, probably like any-where. I know no one and only see the neighbours if we trouve to pass on the communal stairs. I am lonely, on my sel, I must admit.

But once a week, I go down the road into the area office for Her Majesty's Customs and Excise and help with all their kompyuter work in respect of investigating the darknet. I have made them millions, far in excess of the measly £3 million they would have made from me. My conscience is clear. Although I have received threats of violence from the bad men we are chasing down. We have to change our identity on the darknet all the time and I am sure one day they may find me. I am unclear how Mrs D and all her team live with it. But they do, they seem to enjoy it, perversely. A crusade, as such.

Of course, yours candidly has won, as I have all the A Digital Tomato wedge 'clean' and available for my own use. It does not make me happy nor please me. The dosh is just earning interest and a very small sum at that.

Gio, his protest group and his lawyer have long gone. Not a word since my solicitor's letter. Just a spoilt pye trying to make a stir. What a nerd. One who you just have to stomach during lavi. But at the time, very upsetting and disturbing. It went a long way to cause my complete lack of enthusiasm for developing my game which in turn gave so many others such fun. For each and every complaint from someone like Gio I received a thousand comments of praise, but the one moan sticks with you. Sisters, I think you know exactly what I mean. And you all agree with me.

Sally was charged within a week of leaving the hospital and

transferred back to the Midlands. Chief Inspector Pendlebury was promoted within the force. Yes, the cold guys get on. Of course, they do, by bullying mainly. Shameless people. I have no idea how they live with themselves and their consciences. This really depressed me after his unsolicited sexual approach to me that evening while in custody.

I have no idea what has happened to Sir Tim. I took him off all my alerts and I do not care. The let down and lack of trust still haunts me. Politicians are just ugly celebrities. Who cares about them?

Sally's trial was last week. I was allowed to watch via zoom, the defendant and the prosecution can allow winternet visitors these days. Sally approved me. She was found guilty of first-degree murder and sentenced to eighteen years in prison. With good behaviour, this could well be reduced to something like half of the term.

A long time for a twenty-something girl after one night's screw with a screw with a screwdriver. I do not condone it, but hey ho, I am pleased the sentence was limited to this. It seems so long ago now, just looking back. I suppose she took the whole brunt and total burden for any young person fighting against authority. Just her very cold luck. This is the way I think about the episode nowadays.

By the time she is released she will be a different person and probably move abroad. I may give her some wedge then as a starter and nest egg so she can rebuild her life. So sad, but without this help from me what would she be doing in the future, wherever she settles?

For my own fulfilment, I have started the Masters in social behaviour. It is the only thing keeping me going for now. It is great fun and very interesting and rewarding. I should be able to knock off the open university lessons in half the time of a normal degree. Learning a totally different subject away from kompyuters has enabled me to reflect and put in perspective everything I experienced those few days just six months ago. However, I recognize the chapters on depression and anti-social behaviour so clearly, as being me, to a tee. All me.

I still get extremely depressed about it all, the events in Surbiton. A very ripping sonj.

I speak to Pat and Mom once a month and I find their life so dull and boring. Pat is still chofering and can only talk about retirement. Mom is still packing and I still have not asked her what she packs. Perhaps she doesn't even know herself. They seem so distant and unloving. I have to admit, sisters, I know I was and am rejected by them.

About a month ago I went back to the coffeehouse in Surbiton where the donut twins hang out. Luckily, without giving them any notice I did run into them there. I just wanted to see if they had changed. I gave them both £25,000 each as a leave present six months ago. They were pleased and happy but gave me little in the way of thanks, almost as if they expected something. This did not impress me at all.

I could not believe my zyes. Cyril had a girlfriend. Also, she was pregnant. Firstly, I could not see why any female would find him attractive. He is ugly. Nor want any banging with him. Let alone fall with child. Secondly, I felt for their future life,

I was very despondent about it all. A life on Government benefits but I suppose the money I collect for the taxman may go some way to help. Which is one way to look at it. Thirdly, the little child will not have a start in life. In fact, no start at all. It will be undernourished and under-loved. I have no idea what sort of mother his girlfriend will be but looking at her, not much.

I shudder with any further thoughts about them all.

I understand from Pat and Mom they are happy to have a grandchild on the way. I can see them helping out enormously. It may force them to retire. Cyril and his gal mate and the kid, as well as Albie, will be living at home in Surbiton. Pat and Mom spoke to me after I had visited and there was a clear and definite inference at my inability to find a stoodge mate and donnen a baby. This made me feel so inadequate and very, very tearful. Letting people down is a cold feeling, especially if you are sensitive, lonely and miserable. Like me.

When I saw Cyril, Albie was there of course, looking so plum and awkward. I am sure he is not happy, jealous even, about the girlfriend and he is probably trying to find one himself. I am told they have spread out and have a room each. Albie is in my old room, it being the smaller of the two, of course.

I suppose the biggest shock for me when I saw the twins and a real frig is the fact they are both trying to be junior boys in blue. They have applied and are waiting for their interviews. Mom helped them with their application forms and wrote their curriculum vitae for them. They could not have done it themselves. I would be surprised if the feds hire them. Even if they do, they will be career foot fodder constables. Walking the streets and taking the drunks in every Friday and Saturday night, just as they behaved. What a life in store for them. If they are even as successful to be hired.

My depression kicks in again and I decide to lie on the bed. I call the tax office and say I will not be in tomorrow.

I cannot help thinking of my family. Pat is such a good, honest and decent man. He does not deserve the twins, but then I do blame him for not showing any hope or aspiration. It follows generation after generation, for sure. We are all an example to follow. For Mom, the same, just packing and working and trying to provide. An ordinary life for an ordinary person and while it must be admired, I am unclear what she obtains from it. Merely an existence, there must be something to work for rather than the end of the shift or the last box to pack. We are all different and I suppose that is what makes us the same.

I find all this quite upsetting as those who are similar to me and wish to engage with me always think I am super clever. Those who do not, think of me as too smart for my own good.

Quite honestly, I do not know who or what I am at present. I am gubbled, for that, I am sure.

This upsets me immensely. I cry, just as much as I did when I zorted of Sally, my one-time bestie.

The youth have no aspiration nor hope. I always go back to this.

Youth! There is nothing like youth. The middle-aged are mortgaged to life. The old are in life's lumber room. But youth is the Lord of life. Youth has a kingdom waiting for it. Everyone is born a king and most die in exile.

I am in exile now, in Guildford, away from my family. They gave me no comfort while I was living in Surbiton, but after all they were there, just in another room, only a few meters away physically. I have some sleeping and other pills in front of me and a pint of water. I throw the whole of two pots of pills into the water and watch them dissolve. It is a murky, discoloured glass of water now. Some boom, tasty and potent cocktail.

I think of the five-o in the Midlands. Still running riot and doing everything they want. Pushing their authority over everyone. I think of Sally. The eediat therapists trying to persuade me to watch my anger management or to change who I am. They are possibly still operating and doing no good at all. The very cheek of it all.

I look at the pint glass.

A Digital Tomato is still going with everyone, like real life, milling around and getting nowhere. Climbing Levels only to be pushed back down again. The age of information they call it. More like disinformation in my view. How prescient Snakes and Ladders was as a game for the youngsters.

I pick up the pint glass. I do not feel so lonely anymore with this in my hand. I have been ripping, desolate and deserted, but I feel so warm, happy and content now. I have found a solution.

I have made a will from some digital version from the winternet. £1 million left to Pat and Mom and £1 million for my bestie, Sally. Perhaps I do love her. Her new start will be assured, I feel good about that. We all need good bloods. Then the balance of my estate left to the leading mental health charity in the country. That legacy is tax free, I read on the winternet, so this pleases me to no end. I have made a complete list of all the bank accounts I have. Someone else, a good kompyuter hacker, can work out the passwords, if they are required. I love the irony.

Pat and Mom can do what they want with their money. I do not want them to feel any remorse about me. I do not know how I can ditch that feeling about them. I should not worry myself about it either.

Then I think of everyone in the past who suffered. Their torments and troubles. The men in their white coats, practicing on them all as if they were lab rats. I was a test case as an example, too. Sisters, it felt like that, anyway.

Nothing has changed for the better. Apart from the digitalization and instant access to information, social media and communication. Nothing has really changed. Every story from the past was so foreboding of today.

In summary, the youth have not got a fair crack at life. Especially the disadvantaged. At no time will they. It will never ever improve despite all the heavy and well-meaning promises.

I turn off all my fones, my social media. I turn off my kompyuter and all that ting.

I put the glass to my lips. I begin to feel free. Fully relieved, but one last thing.

'That's it.' Groping for some meaningful words, I write on a pad just by my will and leaving them both on the bedside table.

'Good luck to everyone with their individual aspiration and collective hope in this hostile dystopian world. But, please don't be fooled, there are no triumphant dreams and never will be.

Mum and Dad it is not your fault, it's all mine. I had too much expectation.' Then I add on a separate line.

'My answer to all this, changes nothing for everyone but everything for me.'

Sisters, you appreciate I am extremely different, I am ever and always so very successful, so I decide to cancel myself. I put the cocktail drink down on the table next to me ready to drink.

I close my zyes and fall into a deep kabicha.

The metaverse and all its augmented existence appears so palpable.

No uncertainty nor ambiguity and such hope and aspiration for us all.

So, I wake, and knock the glass over, my sisters. To start at Level I, Section I, again. Chargin.

Quotes

Questions on understanding the story

1 State what factors you see in the book which demonstrate Henrietta has a personality disorder?

2 List all the dilemmas and issues which she faces.

3 Which friendship does she hold dear and what is the bond?

4 Describe her family relationships and why they are dysfunctional?

5 Are there any points in the story when you think Henrietta could have changed the outcome?

6 Do you think Henrietta really had the money she boasts about?

7 Do you think Henrietta will now change her ways?

Acknowledgements

I must thank all those I have met, such as those on the five-day residential course with Arvon.

In particular, sincere thanks must go to Dr Todd Swift and his team at Black Spring Press and Eyewear for believing in me and taking me on. Their inspiration, thoughts, directions and above all tremendous intuition have helped me create this story. It was submitted as an uncut diamond, very raw only to be polished, sparkled and glistened to become what it now is.

I sincerely trust you, the readers, have enjoyed it, understood the message and can help in some way to assist today's youth through their lives.

Pidpat glossary (Pidpat to English)

PIDPAT	ENGLISH
achte	buy
afo	aloud
aggie	hit/blow
anpoche	pocket
anreta	remarkable
ansyen	ancient
badman	criminal
bait	immoral
bando	band
bang	making love
bang	sex
bann	gang
bare	lots
barye	barrier
bashment	ragga music
bataying	fighting
bedren	brother
bek	beak
bestie	best friend
bew	drink

bibliotek	library
bill	one £100
biwo	office
bling	chain
bling	jewelry
blood	friend
bloodclot	swear
blues in twos	policeman
boffins	professors
boog	fake
boom	good
bouche	speak/talk
bounce	go
boy in blue	policeman
brass	broke
breeze	easy
brenn	brain
bri	noise
brown	cigarette
bubbles	testicles
buckey	gun
bull	nonsense
bum boclot	swear
bun	smoke
butters	ugly
buzz	drunk
bwoy	boy
cack	worthless
cajun	police officer
cats	crack addict
cha	tea
chante	song

chaps	gold bracelet
chargin	excellent
charitab	generous
chat	cat
chello	person, man
cheve	hair
chick/gal	chick/girl
chofer	drive
chort	laugh
chung	prostitute
cockle	ten pounds
coconut	black/white
cold	bad
cotch	relax
cryptomato	currency
cuss	insult
dam	lady
de	two
dechire	rip
defans	guard
dega	harm/damage
derikson	lead somewhere
det	dig
didgets	telephone no
diet	weak
dillbat	bastard
dis and dat	this and that
diss	abuse
ditch	stop
dizit	say to
dodo	sleep
donnen	produce

donut	stupid
dosh	money
dosye	story
dous	sweet
dowy	mean
draw	drug
drummed	robbery
duck	leave
dunfa	prisoner
dye	god
edge	fifty
eediat	stupid
efreye	frightened
ekole	school
Emarq	digital markets
embesil	fool
epouz	wife
eskelet	skeleton key
eskiz	apology
fache	mad
facht	upset
fat	fat or obese
fed	police officer
fenet	window
fig	fag
fit	attractive
five-o	police officer
flex/head	copulation
fo	loud
fone	phone/mobile/iPhone
fowzy	smelling
fraff	rubbish

fraggle	stupid
frass	tired
frekan	arrogant
frer	friend
frig	kill
gade	look
garms	clothes
gazzy	see/look
glarbies	smart uniforms
gob	throat
grad	graduate
gran	big great
granfem	old woman
granmoun	old man
grill	mouth
grizzle	snout
gubble	confused
gwoup	group
gyaldem	group of girls
gysmos	equipmment
hard hat	helmet
ice	diamond
ital	cigarett marij
itch up	small
jacked	robbed
jacks	five pounds
jakes	police officer
janm	foot, leg
jenn	young
journal	newspaper
jwet	game
kabicha	sleep

kaka	feces/shit
kanon	cannon
kavite	hole
kenbe	caught
kenro	hair braids
kettle	wrist watch
kickers	trainers
klef	key
koko makak	club
kome	woman
kompyuter	computer
konba	battle
konfit	jam
konprann	understand to
konsey	advice
kooba	crack cocaine
kou	neck
koumense	begin
kouto	knife
kreps	trainers
labrish	gossip
lait	milk
lajwa	joy
larenks	voice
lave	wash to
lavi	life
lespri	mind
liklmo	farewell
linets	eyeglasses
lips	to kiss
mache	walk
malen	brainy/clever

mamot	mumble to
mandem	group of men
matou	tomcat
merky	good
monkey	five hund £
moso	piece
mot	word
mouchwa	handkerchief
moun	body
moun	people
moved out	arrested
munch	food
mush	lip
nang	very good
nezzies	underpants
non	name
nugget	pound coin
ochan	cry out
ochan	yowl to
okabine	defecate
panse	thought
pantouf	slippers
paper	money
parans	parents
pat and mom	dad and mum
pata	paw
patat	potato
pawol	filthy
pen	bread
pesky	annoying
pidgin	frivolous
ping	ring tone

pinky	fifty £
plas	place
plum	stupid
pran	grab
presye	dear, valuable
prizon	state jail
punk	anti-establishment
pye	fool
quas	little, tiny
raggo	obvious
ranmase	pick up
rass	buttocks
rass clot	swear
razwa	razor
reach	come
redeye	jealous
rev	chaplain
richi	rich
rinse	wear out
ripping	cold
sache	bag
sal	dirty
san	blood
sarka	sarcastic
scazzy	terrified
score	twenty £
screetch	relax
seckle	settle
seen	yes
sel	lonesome
shochan	shout or scream
sik	sugar

silo	narrow space
sinema	cinema
sisters	you, out there
siye	wipe
skin up	drug
skins	cigarett paper
skratty	girl
skrub	poor
snout	tobacco
soloba	snack
son	sound
sonj	dream
soorted	done
soulye	shoe
sousi	concern
souye	soiled
sovaj	wild
spark	punch
sparked	knock to
stenk	smell
stoke	cook up
stoodge	man
stuch	difficult
swa	night
tang	tongue
tas	cup
tatt	tattoo
tay	waist
tempe	time
teribla	terrible
tet	head
tete	breast

tinedje	teenage
tomato	attractive woman
tonni	naked
totoy	sick
tous	guffaw
tranch	slice
travat	work, job
trip	guts
trouve	happen
tusky	erection
twa	three
twalet	washroom
vach	cow
vant	belly
vit	quick
wapp	whats app
wasteman	worthless person
wedge	money
whip	car
winternet	world wide net
yam	eat
yard	house
yatty	girl
youn	one
zantnay	guts
ze	egg
zepol	shoulder
zonbi	trace ghost
zor	hear, listen
zorey	ear
zorye	pillow
zye	eye

First published in 2022
Eyewear Publishing, an imprint of The Black Spring Press Group
Grantully Road, Maida Vale, London W9
United Kingdom

Cover art @padrondesign
Typesetting User Design, Illustration and Typesetting, UK

ISBN-13 978-1-915406-10-1

Publisher's note: this novel is set in the future, at time of publication,
and the narrator's sense of present and past tense and grammar
is therefore paradoxical by definition – how does one write about
something happening that hasn't happened yet?

A DIGITAL TOMATO

R.M. FRITH

A GENTLE PARODY

THE **BLACK SPRING**
PRESS GROUP

A DIGITAL TOMATO